Andrew Garve

Andrew Garve is the pen name of Paul Winterton (1908–2001). He was born in Leicester and educated at the Hulme Grammar School, Manchester and Purley County School, Surrey, after which he took a degree in Economics at London University. He was on the staff of *The Economist* for four years, and then worked for fourteen years for the *London News Chronicle* as reporter, leader writer and foreign correspondent. He was assigned to Moscow from 1942/5, where he was also the correspondent of the BBC's Overseas Service.

After the war he turned to full-time writing of detective and adventure novels and produced more than forty-five books. His work was serialized, televised, broadcast, filmed and translated into some twenty languages. He is noted for his varied and unusual backgrounds – which have included Russia, newspaper offices, the West Indies, ocean sailing, the Australian outback, politics, mountaineering and forestry – and for never repeating a plot.

Andrew Garve was a founder member and first joint secretary of the Crime Writers' Association.

Andrew Garve

THE
NARROW SEARCH

B E L L

First published in 1957 by Collins

This edition published 2011 by Bello
an imprint of Pan Macmillan, a division of Macmillan Publishers Limited
Pan Macmillan, 20 New Wharf Road, London N1 9RR
Basingstoke and Oxford
Associated companies throughout the world

www.panmacmillan.com/imprints/bello
www.curtisbrown.co.uk

ISBN 978-1-4472-1505-9 EPUB
ISBN 978-1-4472-1504-2 POD

Copyright © Andrew Garve, 1957

The right of Andrew Garve to be identified as the
author of this work has been asserted in accordance
with the Copyright, Designs and Patents Act 1988.

A CIP catalogue record for this book is available from the British Library.

Visit www.panmacmillan.com to read more about all our books
and to buy them. You will also find features, author interviews and
news of any author events, and you can sign up for e-newsletters
so that you're always first to hear about our new releases.

Chapter One

Hugh Cameron had been waiting at the rendezvous on Hampstead Heath for more than an hour when Clare Hunter arrived. He was stretched out under an oak tree at the top of a knoll, his tie loosened and askew, his jacket on the grass beside him. At the sound of a car turning off the road below, he raised his head, but only slightly, as though he no longer had much hope that a new arrival could mean anything to him. When he saw that it was really Clare at last he sat up and waved, and tapped his watch with an air of accusation.

She waved back, and pulled the driving-mirror round, and carefully powdered her face. Then she drew on a pair of brand-new leather gloves, and picked up her bag, and set off up the slope to join him. She was tall for a girl, but beautifully proportioned, and she moved with long, easy strides that were a pleasure to watch. She didn't hurry, for she was wearing a close-fitting jersey suit and a short camel-hair coat slung round her shoulders, which wasn't the sort of outfit anyone would want to rush about in on a warm June morning.

Hugh got up and stretched. He was about thirty—big, and solidly-built, but active-looking—with pleasant, blunt features and laughter lines at the corners of his eyes.

"Come on, poppet," he called, "there's work to be done, you know. Life's not all beer and skittles, worse luck!"

"I'm sorry," Clare said. "Mrs. Dodds rang up at the very last minute to say her Elsie had dropped a flower pot on her toe. That family's full of calamity. I had to spend ages on the phone before I could get a baby-sitter."

"Okay," Hugh said, "excuse accepted! Don't let it happen again, that's all." He smiled disarmingly at her and began to set up his tripod. "How's Christine—all right?"

"Yes, thanks—except that she's teething madly."

He gave a perfunctory nod and bent over his camera, adjusting the lens aperture. He had very delicate hands, unexpected in so large a man.

"You must be frightfully hot in those things," he said, straightening up at last.

"I'm boiling!"

"Why didn't you bring them with you and change in the car?"

"I did think of it, but I decided it would be too public—I've only a bra underneath." Clare threw her shoulders back and put a gloved hand on her hip. "How do I look?"

Hugh regarded her familiar contours with a professional eye. "Nice . . . I wonder if that scarf oughtn't to be pinned a bit higher, perhaps . . . ?"

She smiled at his earnest expression. Once he was on the job, his airy manner dropped from him completely. He became the true artist, intent and dedicated.

"Why not try it and see?" she suggested.

Frowning, he adjusted the big costume brooch at her throat and swept the free end of the silk scarf across her shoulder. "Yes—that's better." He touched her hair, stroking it back to expose a pearl earring.

"Bracelet—or not?" she asked, shielding the thick gold band for a moment with her hand.

"Yes, I think so. Push that sleeve up a bit . . . That's fine."

He stepped back, and surveyed her with pleasure. He had met many lovely women in the course of his illustrating work, but not many of them had Clare's clean-cut beauty. She was a golden brunette, with hair that waved loosely to her shoulders, large brown eyes and facial bones that would have made any photographer reach for his camera. She had lost, perhaps, just a little of the eager vitality she'd had when he'd first met her, four years ago, but she still did pretty well for a married woman of twenty-five with a year-old baby. Anyone who wanted an effect of youth and charm in an outdoor setting would have to go a long way to find a more eye-catching model.

"Well, let's get cracking, shall we?" he said. He explained the proposed lay-out and described the attitude and expression he wanted. Clare, intelligent and co-operative, listened carefully. "I'd like you leaning against the tree first of all. . . ."

The posing and photographing went smoothly, as it almost always did. By now, Hugh knew everything there was to know about Clare's best angles. He knew exactly what light and shade could do to her. He knew just how far the lips should be parted, the eyebrows lifted, the chin tilted, to get the effect he needed. For half an hour, he was completely and happily engrossed in his work.

"Well, I think that's about it," he said at last. He gave Clare a cigarette and lit it for her, and began to pack up his camera and tripod. "By the way, did Lena ring you last night?"

"No."

"She said she was going to. Bagguley's have sent along a golf jacket and I think she wants you for it. She was dreaming up something about a man passing in the background, slightly out of focus but obviously turning round to look at you, and you giving him a provocative glance out of the corner of your eye . . ."

"Like this . . .?" Clare leered at him.

"That's it, exactly. Comes naturally to you girls, doesn't it? *And* you get paid for it as well—there's no justice!" Hugh straightened his tie, and picked up his jacket, and they strolled down to the two parked cars.

"What about a drink at the Spaniards?" he suggested. Clare's face, so lively and carefree until now, clouded a little. "I think I'd better go straight home, Hugh, thanks," she said. "It's getting late, and I haven't done a thing about lunch yet."

He didn't press her. "Right—I'll be seeing you. I'll send the pictures along as soon as they're ready." He held the car door for her, and stood watching her as she drove away.

The Hunters had an attractive house on the outskirts of the Heath. It was detached, and modern, and larger than they needed, but Arnold Hunter had liked it because it had a double garage and was in a well-to-do road where a number of celebrities lived and was the sort of place that impressed the contacts he made in the course of his import-export business. Clare liked the garden, which was big enough to be fun but not big enough to become a chore. There was a fine chestnut tree at the front which provided welcome shade on a warm day and it was here that she had left Christine.

She glanced at the playpen to assure herself that all was well, and said, "How's she been, Evelyn?"

The schoolgirl baby-sitter closed her book. "Very good, Mrs. Hunter, on the whole. Just a little bit fretful now and again, but nothing much."

Clare felt in her handbag for some coins. "Well, thank you very much for helping me out," she said. "Perhaps you wouldn't mind coming in again some time."

She waved as the girl departed on her bicycle and then dropped down beside the playpen. "How's my precious?" she said. Christine beamed, and held out her hands to be picked up. She was an enchanting baby, with her mother's dark eyes and merry smile—a Clare in miniature. Usually she would play on her own for hours, happy and absorbed. To-day she was more demanding. There was a hectic flush on one cheek, and her smile was fleeting and troubled.

Clare gathered her up and nursed her for a few moments, gently massaging the sore gum with her finger. Then, mindful of Arnold's imminent arrival, she reluctantly put her back into the playpen and went indoors to change into a cotton frock and begin preparations for lunch.

She was busy in the kitchen when he came. She listened for a second, trying to sense his mood. She always knew when he was pleased with himself because he would drive in too fast and brake hard, scattering the gravel, and his step in the hall would be brisk and proprietorial. When he was depressed, and full of the self-pity that he showed only to her, he would come in slowly and silently

4

and drop into a chair. To-day, the look on his face suggested worried preoccupation rather than gloom. He hadn't stopped, she realised, even for a moment by the playpen.

She said "Hullo!", turning her cheek passively to receive his kiss. Arnold went almost immediately to the refrigerator to get ice for a drink. He was forty, slim and tall and strikingly handsome, with a film idol's regularity of feature. Except for his vivid blue eyes he was very dark, with thick glossy black hair, strongly-marked eyebrows, and a meticulously-groomed hairline moustache. Everything about him spoke of a loving care for his appearance. Even his sports jacket and flannels, the casual business uniform for Saturday mornings, were impeccably cut.

"Will you have a drink?" he said.

"A very small sherry, please."

He poured it out for her and set it on the table and mixed a large martini for himself. Then he stood eyeing her.

"Well, I put that fellow Granger in his place to-day," he said after a moment.

"Oh?" She knew of Granger as a man in the same line of business as Arnold, though she'd never met him.

"Yes, he had the nerve to tell me how I ought to have handled a consignment. I told him when I wanted his advice I'd ask for it. He didn't like it a bit."

"That's hardly surprising," Clare said.

"It serves him right—he shouldn't be so patronising. I'm damned if I'm going to be talked down to by a little pygmy like Granger." Arnold glanced at his watch, throwing out his arm and baring his strong wrist in a theatrical gesture. "I say, you're a bit behind to-day, aren't you?"

"I am, rather. I've been modelling this morning. The jersey suit—I did tell you about it."

His face took on a disagreeable expression. "It must be nice to be in such demand. That's about the third time this month."

"Oh, these things always come in a rush or not at all."

"Where did you go this time?"

"Only on to the Heath. Hugh met me there."

Arnold grunted. "I don't know how that chap would manage to make a living without you."

"Hugh? Don't be silly. He's a first-class illustrator."

"I wouldn't have said so. What I've seen of his stuff didn't amount to much."

"Perhaps you're not a very good judge," Clare said. "Lena thinks he's brilliant."

"Oh, Lena would gush over any unattached man. If he's as good as all that, why don't any of the big agencies offer him a steady job?"

"But they have. He doesn't want to tie himself down. He prefers being a free-lance."

Arnold finished his drink and poured himself another.

"If you ask me, he just likes lounging about. All these artist fellows are the same—they don't know what real work is."

Clare said expressionlessly, "Would you mind watching those chops, please, while I get Christine? Lunch will be ready in a few minutes."

It wasn't a cheerful meal. Arnold, who could be an exuberant talker when he thought he might be able to make use of someone, or when he'd pulled off a clever deal, or even when he'd merely beaten a rival at golf, now sat in morose silence. Clare concentrated on feeding Christine, ignoring his sour glances. Christine, chuckling and whimpering by turns, preferred for long periods to gnaw her fist. After her spoon had clattered to the floor for the third time Arnold suddenly pushed back his chair and stalked from the table.

When Clare joined him in the sitting-room twenty minutes later he was hunched on the settee, brooding. She poured out his coffee and gave it to him.

"Is anything the matter, Arnold?"

"Not a thing," he growled. "Why should there be?"

"Are you sure?"

"Of course I'm sure."

She stirred her coffee and gazed out of the window. It was a beautiful afternoon. She would have liked to take the car out into

Surrey somewhere and find a high, lonely spot on the Downs with a wonderful view, and lie in the sun, with Christine rolling contentedly on the grass beside her. She looked across at Arnold, but he was still huddled up, absorbed in thoughts that were anything but pleasant, to judge by his expression, and certainly in no mood for an outing. She sighed. Well, there was plenty to do in the garden.

"Did Chappell say anything about having some chrysanthemum plants for me?" she asked.

Arnold glanced up sharply. "No, he didn't."

"I just wondered—he said they'd be ready this week-end. Perhaps you'd ask him about them on Monday?"

Arnold reached for a cigarette and flicked his gold lighter on with a snap. "He won't be coming on Monday."

"Oh!—why? He's not ill, is he?"

"He's left the firm."

"Left the firm! *Chappell!*"

"Yes, I've pensioned him off. I decided he'd been around long enough."

Clare gazed at him in astonishment. "But, Arnold, he's not nearly ready for a pension. He can't be a day more than fifty-five."

"His age is beside the point. He's been behaving like a doddering old fool and I can't put up with him any longer."

"But—I don't understand. You always said he was so useful."

"Well, as far as I'm concerned he's outlived his usefulness. He can't even keep his files straight. I wanted some papers to show Mathieson the other day, and when Chappell brought them in they were all mixed up and I couldn't make head or tail of them. Mathieson said I was wasting his time, and went off in a huff. I just can't afford that sort of thing."

"No, of course not, but ... What did Chappell say?"

"He said he was sorry. Sorry! Why, a child of ten could keep those few papers in order."

"It sounds most extraordinary—he was always so proud of the way he kept his files. .... In any case, Arnold, it's hardly fair to get rid of a man simply because of one blunder."

"Oh, I've had trouble with him before. ...." Arnold picked up the midday paper and opened it with a crackle. "And really, I can't see why you have to concern yourself about him."

"Chappell happens to be rather a friend of mine, that's all."

"What, because he gives you a few plants?"

"No . . . He's a nice little man, and sweet to Christine—I like him."

"All I can say is, you make friends of the queerest people."

"At least my friends aren't shifty," Clare said her eyes bright with anger. "I thought that man you brought in for a drink last week was perfectly horrible—*and* there've been others like him. I don't know how you can stand them."

"In business," said Arnold, "you can't pick and choose—you have to deal with all sorts."

"Then it's a pity I only seem to see the one sort. . . ." With an effort, she controlled her rising temper. "What pension are you giving Chappell?"

"Five pounds a week—and if he's not grateful, he ought to be. I could have sacked him out of hand for inefficiency. There aren't many employers who would be so generous."

"All the same," said Clare after a moment, "I don't see how he'll live on it. Everything costs so much now, and I don't believe he's finished buying his house yet. . . ."

"That's his affair. I don't run my business as a charity, and if people let me down they must take the consequences. He'll have to get another job."

"At fifty-five?"

"He'll find something—they always do. Any fool can earn a living these days."

"Well, I think you're treating him abominably. Everybody makes mistakes sometimes, and he has been with the firm all his life. . . ."

"Not with me, he hasn't."

"He was with Holt's, and you bought out Holt's, so he became your responsibility. And nobody could have been more loyal and conscientious. . . ."

"Good God, Clare, you talk as though he'd been the mainstay of the firm! What is he, after all?—just a grown-up office boy who's been kept on because he knows where to find the string and sealing-wax and doesn't mind running errands and making the tea and doing the dogsbody jobs. Actually, the fellow's a complete nitwit."

"Well, I wish you'd give him another chance. Please, Arnold—won't you?"

"I can't—it's all settled. He's had a month's pay in lieu of notice, and he's gone. And I'd much prefer it, Clare, if you didn't meddle in these things."

Silently, Clare gathered up the coffee-cups and carried them into the kitchen.

Albert Chappell was mowing the front lawn of his modest, semi-detached villa in Mill Hill when Clare drove up to the gate that afternoon. For a moment he stared at the car in surprise. Then he put on his jacket and hurried out into the road. He was an active shrimp of a man, with ruddy cheeks and mild accommodating eyes, and sparse grey hair. "Hullo, Mrs. Hunter," he said, and smiled down at Christine, who was strapped in a chair over the passenger seat and was ogling him shamelessly.

"Hallo," said Clare. "You're very busy for a warm day."

"Got to keep the place nice," he said.

"It looks lovely ... Mr. Chappell, I had to come and tell you how terribly sorry I am about the job. I've only just heard."

"It's very kind of you," he said.

"It's so completely unexpected."

"Yes," he said, his face clouding. "It's been a great shock—no good pretending it hasn't. Specially for the wife."

"Is Mrs. Chappell at home?"

"No. She' s gone to the pictures—trying to take her mind off things. She worries, you know. I keep telling her there's lots of folks would think themselves lucky to get a good pension at my age, but she doesn't see it that way."

"I'm sure you don't, either."

"Well, it's not very nice being got rid of like that—makes you feel you've not been any use to anybody. Seems as though it's all been a waste. ..."

9

"You mustn't feel like that, Mr. Chappell, because you know it's not true. . . ." Clare hesitated. "I wish there was something I could do. I did wonder if perhaps you'd not been feeling quite yourself lately. You see, if you hadn't been well, or if you'd had something bothering you, I could explain that to my husband."

Albert shook his head. "I've been right as rain, Mrs. Hunter. Never felt better."

"Oh, dear. Tell me, how did it happen? About the files, I mean. Was it just one of those things?"

"I'm blessed if I know," he said ruefully. "That one I gave Mr. Hunter was in such a mess I thought maybe young William had been playing about with it, just for a lark, but he says he didn't, and he's a good lad. He wouldn't tell me what wasn't true, specially when he knew I was in a fix."

"I'm sure he wouldn't. It is odd, though, isn't it . . . ? When was the last time it happened?"

Albert looked surprised. "Oh, it only happened the once, Mrs. Hunter."

"Really? But I understood from my husband there'd been trouble before."

"No, not over the files."

"Over something else?"

"Well—Mr. Hunter was very angry with me back in February, but that was a different thing."

"What was it?"

"Oh, it wasn't much, really. I'd got a bit behind-hand with some packing, and it was Mrs. Chappell's night for the Guild, so I stayed on a bit at the office to clear up after the others had gone home, and Mr. Hunter didn't like it."

"You mean he didn't like you doing extra work?"

"No, it wasn't that. . . ." Albert looked embarrassed. "You see, he'd got a man with him in his room, and he didn't know I was there, and when he came out and found me he seemed to think I'd been—well, listening."

"Good heavens! Did he say that?"

"Yes, he did. You see, I'd been along for a wash—that's how it was he didn't know I was there when he came in with this man. And then when I was getting my hat and coat he came out and saw me. And it was then he said I'd been listening. Well, of course, I hadn't been able to help hearing a few words, but it wasn't intentional . . . Anyway, next day he said he was sorry for being so sharp, and explained it all."

"What did he explain?"

"Well, what I'd heard. . . ." Albert said uneasily.

"I see." Clare looked at him for a moment, then suddenly leaned forward and pressed the starter button.

"Well, give my regards to Mrs. Chappell and tell her not to worry too much."

"I will, Mrs. Hunter . . . Wouldn't you like to take those chrysanths while you're here? They're all ready."

"Are they?" She was anxious to get home, now, but she didn't want to hurt him. "All right, then, if it's no trouble. Thank you."

"I won't be a minute." Albert scurried up the narrow concrete path and through the back gate to his greenhouse. He re-emerged almost at once with a wooden box filled with neat rows of chrysanthemum plants, each row methodically labelled for colour. He spread a sheet of brown paper carefully over the back seat and arranged the box so that it wouldn't jolt or chafe anything. "There!" he said.

Clare, watching him, thought again how extraordinary it was that Chappell, the orderly, conscientious Chappell, should have got his files mixed up. The last man in the world, she would have said.

. . .

Arnold was out when she got home. She gave Christine her tea, and bathed her, and had just put her to bed when he came in.

"Oh, you're back," he said. "You slipped off very quietly this afternoon."

"Yes," she said. "I went to see Chappell."

"Chappell!" He turned on her in a fury, and for one incredible moment she thought he was going to hit her. "How dare you!"

Clare looked at him coldly. "Don't talk to me like that, Arnold—I'm not one of your employees."

"You'd no right to go. I told you not to interfere."

"I had to go. I thought he might have been ill, or something. I went to see if there was anything I could do."

She sat down, and lit a cigarette. "Arnold, there's something I want to ask you ... When you found Chappell working late in the office one evening last February and accused him of eavesdropping—what exactly were you up to?"

Anger blazed in his eyes again. "My God, you're a fine, loyal wife, I must say. I get rid of a man because he's an incompetent fool, and you rush off and gossip with him behind my back."

"I didn't gossip with him," she said. "It was quite by chance that the incident came up."

"There wasn't any 'incident' to speak of."

"Well, whatever there was, I'd like to know about it. Who was the man you were talking to, and what was it all about?"

"I refuse to discuss it."

Clare said: "Arnold, I'm not going to be kept in the dark any longer. I'm worried about you—and about the business. I have been for a long time. I don't like the people you mix with."

"Pure prejudice!"

"If it is, reassure me. What were you so afraid Chappell might hear?"

"Nothing that's any concern of yours."

"Very well, I didn't press Chappell for details, because I hoped I'd hear them from you, but if you're going to take this attitude I shall obviously have to ask him."

Arnold stared at her for a long moment. Then he dropped into a chair opposite her. "Now look here, Clare," he said in a placatory tone, "you're worrying yourself about nothing. I'm not really trying to keep anything from you—it's just that I don't like being badgered about trifling business matters. This affair over Chappell—it didn't amount to a thing ... The fact is, I'd been out having a drink with Arthur Peebles, and I brought him back to the office about seven to show him some samples he was interested in. I took him into my room, and he had a look at the stuff, and we talked for a bit, and suddenly I heard someone moving in the corridor. Well, it was late, and it's pretty lonely down there by the canal, and I thought someone must have broken in. I pulled open the door, and there was old Chappell. I was completely taken aback, and I told him he'd no business to be hanging around at that hour, and packed him off home. I know it was idiotic to accuse him of listening, but I was very annoyed at the time. I said I was sorry afterwards, though—and that's all there is to it."

"Is it . . . ? I understand from Chappell that he did hear something as he came down the passage, and that you *explained* it all the next day. What was there to explain?"

"For heaven's sake, Clare, do I have to be cross-examined like this?"

"It seems the only way to get anything out of you."

"But it's all so trifling . . . If you must know, Peebles and I were discussing a case that had been in the papers. It was about some chaps who'd shipped stuff behind the Iron Curtain without a licence. I knew Chappell must have heard us talking, and I thought he might get hold of the wrong end of the stick, so next day I had him in and explained that it was just a newspaper story we'd been talking about."

"Was that necessary?"

"Well, I didn't want him getting any peculiar ideas and imagining that *we* were mixed up in anything like that."

There was a little silence. Then Clare, very pale, said, "I'm sorry, Arnold, but I'm afraid I don't believe you."

"Why not?" he said sharply. "It's the truth."

She shook her head. "It doesn't make sense to me. I don't believe anyone with a clear conscience would have bothered to explain. I don't think it made sense to Chappell, either. He's very loyal, and he's tried to convince himself that he didn't hear what he thought he heard, but he hasn't succeeded . . . Arnold, don't you see that we can't leave things like this? If you won't be frank with me I shall go to Chappell again. I simply have to know."

There was another long pause. Arnold's face wore a resentful, trapped expression. Clare waited, outwardly calm.

At last he said, "All right, Clare—I'll tell you. It's about time I shared the burden, anyway. The fact is, I've been in a bit of a jam ... You see, last winter Arthur Peebles came to me with an idea for shipping some aluminium to Poland, and he asked me if I'd help to finance the deal. As it happened, I'd just had one or two bad breaks, so it was a tempting proposition. I rather wish now that I'd told him to go to hell, but he seemed a smart chap and he'd got it all worked out very cleverly and in the end I said I'd join in. So he went ahead, and pulled it off, and I got a nice cut—several thousand. I don't mind telling you if it hadn't been for that you wouldn't have had your new car in the spring. ...'

"Go on," Clare said.

"Well, that evening when Chappell stayed late we were sort of celebrating. I knew Chappell must have heard something, but I didn't worry too much about it because he's pretty stupid and anyway he accepted my explanation ... Then, last week, things suddenly started to go wrong. Peebles must have slipped up somewhere, because a couple of nosy officials called at his place and started asking questions and it looks as though he may be in the soup. It could even mean jail for him. Of course, they may not find anything, and even if they do they won't get around to me—you can be sure I took good care to cover up—so there's nothing to worry about. The whole thing's a scandal, really—after all, it isn't as though we were doing anything dishonest, we were only trying to get around a lot of damfool regulations and red tape ... Still, you can see why I couldn't keep Chappell on—if there were ever any inquiries at the office, he'd be just the sort of idiot to give the show away without even realising what he was doing. I'm sorry I had to push him off in such a hurry, but I've given him as good a pension as I dare without being suspiciously generous, and I might even be able to take him back in the end, when things have blown over. ...."

"Arnold—did *you* fix those files?"

He hesitated, then nodded. "I didn't enjoy doing it, but once I'd decided he'd got to go I had to find some reason."

"How *could* you?"

"I don't see that it's made any difference to him. He'd have had to leave, anyway."

Clare got up and walked slowly into the hall. Arnold followed her. "I'm sorry about all this, Clare," he said, "but it's the kind of thing that does happen, and there's no real harm done if we keep our heads ... Where are you going?"

"Out," she said "Just out!"

It was Arnold's custom to play eighteen holes on fine Sunday mornings, and next day, greatly to Clare's relief, he went off to the club-house immediately after breakfast as though nothing unusual had happened. He had not referred again to their conversation of the previous evening, and neither had she. As soon as he had gone she strapped Christine into the car and drove off to see Lena Howell.

Lena lived in a spacious mews flat off Knightsbridge. She was a career woman, a group-head in a prosperous advertising firm, and considerably older than Clare. Worldly and shrewd where her job was concerned, she was fundamentally good-natured, and she had a particular fondness for Clare. She had given her her first modelling engagements as a beginner; and when, a year or two back, business had taken Clare's people to Singapore to live, Lena had considered herself as having been left *in loco parentis*. That, in practice, meant that she felt specially privileged to bully her if the need arose—which in Lena's opinion happened quite often. She was drinking coffee, voluptuous-looking in a gorgeous dressing-gown, when Clare arrived.

"Heavens!" she exclaimed, "what on earth are you doing here on a Sunday morning? No roast and two veg. for your lord and master to-day?"

Clare smiled wanly. Lena gave her a sharp look and said, "Have some coffee. And put that child down. You'll throw your hip out holding her like that. Spoil your line."

Clare put Christine on the floor and gave her some toys to play with. "Well, what's up?" Lena said.

Clare looked at her friend unhappily, "Lena—I think I'll have to leave Arnold."

"Oh." Lena reached for a cigarette and lit it. "Well, I can't honestly say I'm surprised. What's precipitated this crisis, may I ask?"

"Something rather frightful, actually. . . ." Clare hesitated. "I suppose I oughtn't to be talking about this at all, because it could lead to awful trouble, but I've simply got to get it off my chest . . . Do you think you could manage to forget what I've said, afterwards?"

Lena smiled grimly. "Go ahead," she said, "I'll forget whatever you want me to forget."

"Well, the thing is, Arnold's in some kind of mess at the office. I don't quite understand it, but apparently he and some other men have been doing something illegal, and if it were found out I think he might be sent to prison. . . ." Briefly, she told Lena what she knew.

"Good lord!" Lena said, as she finished. "*What* a fool!"

"I've been half-expecting it for ages, as a matter of fact. I've had a feeling for a long time that the business wasn't quite straight. He's been so cagey about it always, and so angry if I ever asked questions."

"What's his attitude now?"

"Well, in the first place that there's nothing to worry about because nothing will be found out. And in the second place, according to him he's done nothing wrong. As long as he's not caught—that's all he cares about. And that's what frightens me. If he'd simply made one foolish mistake—given way to sudden temptation, that sort of thing—and was sorry about it and needed me, I'd probably feel quite differently about him. I certainly wouldn't leave him in the lurch. But that's not his attitude at all. He seems to think he's perfectly entitled to get away with anything he can. I suppose I must have known it for a long time subconsciously, but I've never really faced it until now—he simply hasn't got the same sort of moral sense as most people."

"It makes the outlook pretty grim, doesn't it?" Lena said.

"Well, that's just the point. You see, if he gets away with it this time, he's bound to be worse than ever—and where's it going to end? It's Christine I'm worried about. What's going to happen to her if she grows up with that sort of background? And that isn't all, either. You know how I've always looked forward to having what I call a proper family, a nice big one, but now the thought of having any more of Arnold's children makes my blood run cold ... Lena, I simply can't go on living with him any more. It's been ghastly for months—this thing at the office is only the last straw. Every time he comes anywhere near me I feel myself freeze."

"I think it's amazing you've stuck it so long," Lena said.

"I ought never to have married him in the first place, I suppose. I didn't even begin to know what he was like."

"Does anyone ever?"

"Oh, surely ... ? But I certainly didn't. I must have been mad."

"Not mad, angel, just crazily in love. It's not surprising. There he was—tall, dark and handsome, nice line in talk, experienced, plenty of money. And that twisted mind of his well out of sight. He'd have swept any girl off her feet. You were only twenty-two, after all. That's not much of an age to make the decision of a lifetime, is it?"

Clare sighed. "All the same, it's pretty humiliating to know one's made such a hash of things. I never doubted it would work out all right—he talked with such confidence about everything. Do you remember how I admired him because he'd struggled out of his background and wasn't going to let anything beat him? What a fool I was! He's so arrogant, Lena—and he's got much worse lately. He seems to look on himself as some sort of superman. He's always running other people down and saying beastly things about them and gloating because he's been smart and done someone in the eye. It's not surprising he doesn't make any real friends. And he can't talk about anything except how much money he's making, and what he's going to buy when his next big deal comes off. It's horrible."

"You don't have to convince me," Lena said. "I think he's a case—I've thought so for a long time. He started off with a chip on his shoulder and he's been over-compensating ever since, and once things started going really wrong I wouldn't put anything past him. He's got a warped outlook and a nasty vindictive temper, and I don't trust him an inch."

There was a moment's silence. Then Clare said: "You know, Lena, when you talk like that I feel I ought to be sorry for him, and in a way I am, but I can't see that there's anything I can do. Perhaps it's partly because he's so much older than I am, but I don't seem to have any influence over him at all. When he's trying to appear strong and self-reliant he won't listen to anyone's opinion and he can't stand a breath of criticism—and when he does seem to need me it's only as an audience to hear how depressed he is, and he goes on just the same afterwards."

"In any case," Lena said, "you can't go on living with a man who makes you freeze, just because you're sorry for him. Even a nurse doesn't have to sleep with the patient!"

"No. . . ." Clare said.

"I should move out, Clare, if *I* were you—really, I should. You'll only mess up your life if you stay, and probably Christine's as well. It isn't as though you're dependent on him—you'll be able to earn quite a decent living once you get into your stride again."

"Yes—thank goodness I listened to you and didn't let the modelling drop altogether. Arnold's always hated it, you know—he's resented my having any interest apart from himself, even when he knew I was being left alone a lot. As it is, it shouldn't take me too long to get back where I was . . . I'll have to find someone to look after Christine, of course, while I'm actually on the job, but it isn't even as though I'll be working regular office hours. . . .Oh, well, I suppose I'd better start looking round for a flat or something."

"Why don't you come here for a week or two while you're settling things?" Lena said. "It may not be too easy to find a place right away, and you'll have quite enough worries to be going on with. There's stacks of room here."

"Oh, I don't know, Lena. . . ."

"I mean it, really. I'm out most of the time, after all, and the

Park's very handy for Christine, and the mews gets a lot of sun—it'll be just right for the pram."

"Would you honestly not mind?"

"I would honestly like it very much. Besides—as Christine's godmamma I've a right to a say in her upbringing, and I think it's time she came under the influence of a pure-souled, high-minded woman like me!"

Clare laughed shakily. "It would certainly make things a lot simpler."

"It'll give you a breathing space. Time to think things out a bit on your own. You can come any time. To-day, if you like."

"Well, all right, Lena. Thanks very much. I'll pack up and come to-morrow—it'll be easier when Arnold's out of the way."

"Have you said anything to him yet?"

"Not yet."

"H'm! Well, if you take my advice you'll find some place to break it to him where there are a lot of other people around. His ego's going to take a nasty knock over this, and he isn't going to like it."

"No," said Clare unhappily, "I'm afraid he isn't going to like it at all."

It was just after twelve next day when Arnold's taxi turned into the Park. Already the best bits of shade were occupied by office workers, sprawling contentedly with sandwiches and newspapers. In a moment or two he caught sight of Clare, sitting in a deck chair under a small plane tree. He dismissed the taxi, and strode rapidly towards her.

"Really, Clare," he said in a tone of exasperation as he joined her, "was this necessary? I had to cancel a lunch date because of your message. *And* cross half London."

"I've something important to tell you."

He flung himself down in the chair beside her. "Well, what is it?"

"I'm afraid this is going to sound very abrupt, Arnold, but I don't know any easy way of telling you. . . .The fact is, I'm not going to live with you any more."

His head jerked round, and for a moment he stared at her incredulously. "You can't be serious!"

"I've never been more serious in my life."

"But this is ridiculous. Look, Clare, I know you were upset by that bit of trouble at the office. . . ."

"It's not that," she said. "At least, that's only part of it. I don't love you any more, Arnold. I haven't done for a long time. I'd have thought you would have known by now."

"But—this is fantastic!" he said. "I simply don't believe it. Why, Clare—*why?*"

She sighed. "I suppose it wouldn't be possible for you just to accept the fact?"

"Of course I can't accept it. You must have some reason. What's come over you?"

"There isn't any *one* reason. . . .Arnold, please understand that I'm not trying to put all the blame on you. It's partly my fault for rushing into marriage as I did. It was very stupid—I see that now. The fact is, we've never been right for each other. We've absolutely nothing in common—we look at everything in different ways. . . ."

"I wouldn't say so. What, for instance?"

She gave a little shrug. "Well—take what's happened at the office. As I say, that isn't the whole reason why I'm leaving you, but it is symptomatic of our different outlooks. You call it 'a bit of trouble,' you brush it aside as though it's of no importance, as though it's the kind of thing that happens every day. But I'm appalled."

"That's only because you don't understand these things. Why, it's scarcely more than a technical point. Heavens, if business men always stuck to the letter of these damn silly regulations there'd be no work done at all."

Clare shook her head. "You see what I mean about looking at things differently," she said. "'It's just a technical point!' You'd do it again, wouldn't you, if you thought you could get away with it? *You* say it's not dishonest, but I think it is—horribly. I loathe the atmosphere you work in—all the smart-aleck deals and shady contacts and beastly money-grubbing. I loathe the way you treat people who can't stand up for themselves—people like Chappell. I think you're unjust and—savage. I can't bear it any more. I can't bear it for myself, and I'm going to see that Christine never has to. Arnold, for heaven's sake let's not argue about it—we shall only end up with a scene. I've made up my mind and nothing will alter it."

"And what about *my* mind?" said Arnold. "You can't just walk out on me after all this time. I need you, Clare—I'd be lost without you. The bottom would fall right out of my life. I tell you, it's absolutely unthinkable."

"I'm afraid you'll have to get used to it," she said.

"I never realised you could be so hard."

"I'm sorry—I don't mean to be."

"But you are being." Arnold's voice took on a plaintive note. "And damned ungrateful for all I've done. It's easy for you to take a high moral attitude when all you've had to do is stay at home and wait for the cash to roll in. You can't imagine how I've slaved at that office, year after year. It hasn't been easy, you know, building it up from almost nothing. Perhaps I have been a bit too keen on making a lot of money, but I know what it means not to have it. It's all very well for you—you've never had to struggle up out of squalor. You've always been sheltered. You had a decent home, and security, and a good education, and friends who liked you. You don't know what it feels like not to be wanted, not to have anyone who cares about you. I've had to fight every inch of the way. . . .My God, Clare, when I think of the things I've had to struggle against, the handicaps, the setbacks, I sometimes wonder how I've managed to keep going at all, let alone do as well as I have. And all I get in return is criticism and contempt." Tears of self-pity welled up in his eyes.

"I know it hasn't been easy for you," Clare said, "but it doesn't alter the fact that I'm not the right wife for you."

"But you are, Clare. You are because it's you I want. I rely on you, and you belong to me. You can't *really* mean you want to leave me?"

"I *have* left you," she said.

He was suddenly very still. "What do you mean?"

"I moved into Lena's flat this morning. I'm going to stay there for a week or two and then find somewhere else to live."

"You cleared out without even telling me?"

"It seemed the best way. There would only have been a frightful row if I'd started to pack while you were there—you know there would."

"My God, this is intolerable . . . ! What am I going to do—have you thought of that? I suppose you don't care?"

"Of course I care. I thought you'd probably stay at your club for a bit. But I'll help you to get settled somewhere else if you want me to—I'll help you in any way I can. I don't want to quarrel, Arnold, and I don't see why we should. Other people manage to arrange these things fairly amicably."

"Amicably! You knock the bottom out of my life—*you*, the one person in the world I had a right to count on—and you talk of arranging things amicably! I suppose you think I'll offer to share everything with you if you talk nicely? You've got a hope! And what about Christine—what amicable arrangement have you in mind for her?"

"You'll be able to see her whenever you want to, of course—*if* you want to. You've never bothered much about her before."

"If I haven't, it's because I've been too busy earning your living. That'll stop now, anyway—you won't get another penny out of me if I can help it."

"I don't want anything. I'd like my personal things from the house, that's all. I'll manage, somehow."

"You think you're mighty clever, don't you? You think you've got everything beautifully arranged to suit your own convenience. Next thing, I suppose, you'll be deciding you'd like to divorce me and marry someone else . . . By God, Clare, you certainly don't know me! I'm not a man you can throw aside just when you think you will. You don't know what you're up against. I warn you, you're not going to get away with this. You married me for better or worse, and you're damn well going to stick to your contract."

The venom in his voice appalled her. "Don't be absurd," she said. "You can't *make* me live with you."

"We'll see," said Arnold.

After that conversation she quite expected some positive move on his part, a stiff lawyer's letter at the very least—but nothing happened. He remained stubbornly uncooperative, and that was all. When she telephoned him a couple of days later and suggested that they should meet again and try to discuss the whole position rationally, he asked her sharply if she'd changed her mind and when she told him she hadn't he said there was nothing else he wanted to discuss, and hung up.

He had not, she soon discovered, moved to his club; though he was having all his meals out, he was still sleeping at the house. Each time she visited it, to collect more of her belongings, to pick up her correspondence, to pay Mrs. Dodds, she found a worse state of confusion, as though he were deliberately trying to produce anarchy in the place and so demonstrate his helpless need of her. He had not, it appeared, left any instructions for the tradesmen; nor had he seen or communicated with Mrs. Dodds at all. Clare had to explain to her what had happened, and urge her to carry on for a bit until the situation became clearer. It seemed obvious that before long, if Arnold's attitude didn't change, he would have to be left to cope with things on his own, but Clare hated the feeling that disorder had followed her departure and for the moment she could not escape a sense of continuing responsibility. Sometimes she half wished that she had tried to reach some understanding with him about the future before she had walked out, but—as Lena said—it wasn't likely he would ever have agreed to anything, and they would merely have led a cat-and-dog life, with the same result in the end.

In any case, she had far too much to do to dwell for long on Arnold's unhelpful attitude. In the mornings, after the baby chores were done, she usually put Christine out in the pram and left her in the care of Mrs. Teeling, Lena's daily help, for an hour or two, while she looked around for a permanent place to live. It proved a most dispiriting task. The rents asked were staggering, and though she had a certain amount of money of her own she knew it would probably be some time before she was earning at her full capacity again. She resolutely put out of her mind the houseful of carefully chosen furniture and equipment that she'd left behind at Hampstead, and tried to reconcile herself to the idea of building up a new home out of nothing in a modest couple of rooms. But even those were not easy to find at the right price. Lena's view was that she was being absurdly quixotic in not wanting to take anything from Arnold, and that she had a perfect right to a part of the joint property. But on that point, Clare was adamant. By asking for nothing, she felt, by simply removing herself from an intolerable relationship without making any demands, she was reducing to a minimum Arnold's right to reproach her. If it had been possible, she would have preferred to give rather than receive. From time to time she renewed her efforts to reach some basis of understanding with him, but always without any response. Once, she suggested over the phone that he might care to call round and see Christine, but he replied curtly that he was too busy.

Apart from house-hunting, and Arnold, it was work and the prospect of work that mainly occupied her thoughts. She had lost no time in visiting her former agent and getting her name put back on the register as a full-time model, and already in the first week she had had two very good engagements. Hugh Cameron, who knew many influential people in the business, was also letting it be known as widely as possible that she was available once more, and on several evenings he dropped in at the flat to see how things were going. He had had little to say about her decision to leave Arnold, beyond indicating that he was entirely with her, but his practical help had been worth any amount of personal sympathy. Lena, too, had rallied round with several useful ideas. By now she had finished her layout for the golf jacket, and Hugh suggested an early photographing session in Hyde Park. Next day, therefore—a Friday—Clare left Christine as usual in Mrs. Teeling's charge, and walked across the park to meet him by the Serpentine. The morning was brilliantly sunny, and the park was gay and full of life. The lake was dotted with boats, the horse-riders were active, the nannies were out in strength, the green grass was vividly splashed with colourful summer frocks. It was an exhilarating scene, and Clare's spirits were high. She and Hugh had a lot of fun carrying out Lena's ideas, with Hugh himself acting the passer-by who was to get the provocative look, and when they'd finished he declared himself very satisfied with the morning's work. Afterwards they strolled across to the open-air restaurant and had coffee at a table in the sun, and talked lively shop, and Clare was happy because she felt she was really beginning to get into the professional swim again. She walked back to the flat in the most cheerful frame of mind she'd known since she'd left Arnold a fortnight before.

As she turned into the mews, she saw with surprise that the pram outside the door was empty. She quickened her step—it wasn't usual for Mrs. Teeling to have to take Christine inside. . . .Then, as she reached the pram, she noticed a slip of paper pinned to the pillow, and snatched it up in sudden fear.

It was a note from Arnold, and it read, "I have taken Christine. If you still want to discuss things I am ready to talk to you now."

Chapter Two

Clare had been waiting for hours at the Hampstead house. She had hurried there straight from Lena's flat, sick with anxiety, praying that Arnold had merely taken Christine home; but she found the place deserted. She had telephoned his office and learned that he hadn't been in to work that morning and that no one had any idea where he might be. She had called on Mrs. Dodds, but the charwoman had seen nothing of him for days.

He had his car with him, as well as Christine—that was the one fact she'd had to go on. But she couldn't begin to imagine where he'd gone, or what he was doing. All she knew was that she must stay there now until he returned. She had tried to ring Lena and tell her what had happened, but Lena had been out at some conference.

The afternoon had crawled by. Unable to sit still, Clare had wandered miserably from room to room, stubbing out half-smoked cigarettes, gazing blankly out of the windows, listening for the sound of Arnold's car. Several times she had walked to the gate and stood looking up and down the road for minutes on end. At five she made herself a cup of tea, using up a little time, telling herself he was bound to come soon. But at six there was still no sign of him, and now she could scarcely control her rising panic. This was the time she should have been bathing Christine, tucking her up in her cot with her teddy bear, kissing her good night. . . .

As seven o'clock approached she tried again to get Lena on the phone, this time at the flat. She had just dialled when she heard a car turn in at the gate and stop with a slither of locked wheels on gravel. Arnold! In a flash she was out in the drive, hope surging wildly. He *must* have brought her back—there was nothing else he could have done. . . .But one glance inside the car shattered the hope. She turned and rushed upon him, tugging at his coat lapels with frenzied fingers.

"Arnold, where's Christine? What have you done with her?"

He looked down at her with a satisfied smirk. "Take it easy," he said. "We've plenty of time."

She beat at his chest. "Arnold, tell me! Where is she?"

"In a nice safe place."

"Oh—how can you be so callous! Can't you imagine how I feel?"

"She's all right, I tell you." He turned to go into the house.

"But, Arnold—she should be in bed now. Where have you taken her? She hasn't even a nightie. . . ."

"She's being looked after, don't worry. You're not the only woman in the world, you know."

Clare gave a choking sob. "How *could* you take her—you'd no right."

"Had you any right to take her from me?"

"But she's so young—she needs me. Arnold, please, *please* give her back to me. Tell me where she is."

"You'll have her back soon enough," he said. "There's no need to get upset. I'm sorry I had to be so drastic, but you brought it on yourself. You couldn't possibly have supposed I was going to sit back and do nothing—I did warn you."

"I would never have believed you could do anything so cruel."

"Wasn't it cruel of you to leave me?"

"It's not the same."

"Not to you, perhaps. . . .Anyway, we won't argue about that now. The position's quite simple. You want Christine back—and I want you back. All you have to do is come and live with me again and we shall both get our wish."

"I can't . . . I told you, I've no feeling left for you at all."

"I want you back on any terms—and I'm going to have you." Suddenly he took a step forward and seized her by the shoulders and pulled her roughly towards him, as much in malice as desire.

27

"I won't give you up—do you understand? You're my wife, and you're going to stay my wife."

She struggled fiercely, turning her face away, and in a moment he relaxed his grip and let her go.

"You're mad," she said, backing away and gazing at him almost in fear. "Do you think you can force me to love you? I *hate* you."

"You'll change your tune," he said.

"No!"

"Oh, yes, you will—you'll be on your knees to me before long. You're coming back to me, Clare, if I have to make it my life's work. Nobody's going to treat me as you've treated me and get away with it."

"So that's it," she said, "It's your pride that's hurt." She made an effort to speak calmly. "Arnold, don't be a fool. I'll never be any good to you—you'll be better off without me. It isn't as though you've any love for me, either—if you had, you couldn't do this. I'm just a possession to you. . . .Now tell me where Christine is."

"I'll tell you when you come back to me."

"I shall go to the police, then."

He gave a short laugh. "You'll find they won't be interested. She's my child as much as yours. They'll simply advise you to come back and talk it over."

"I don't believe it," Clare said uncertainly. "I'm her mother—they'll never let you keep her."

"They can't stop me. You forget that possession's nine points of the law. You don't even know where she is—so what can they do?"

She gazed at him in anguish, searching his face for some trace of pity, some weakening of resolve. But his eyes were hard, his mouth was set, and she knew that it was hopeless. Suddenly she turned and rushed from the house.

Hugh Cameron said in a startled voice, "But it's positively inhuman!" He had been called to the flat by Lena to give aid and comfort in the emergency, but the sight of Clare's distress had thrown him temporarily off balance. He paced up and down, a bewildered frown on his face, for once at a loss for words.

"It's just the sort of thing he would do," Lena said furiously. "We knew the man was vicious—we ought to have thought of it."

"Where *could* he have taken her?" Hugh said. "How about his relatives, Clare?"

Clare shook her head. "He hasn't seen any of his family for years. He told me he didn't get on with them." Her voice broke. After the nerve-racking wait at Hampstead, the unproductive wrangle with Arnold, she was clearly on the edge of collapse.

"The thing is," said Lena, "no decent person would take in a twelve-months-old baby just on the husband's say-so, especially if she was brought along without a bib to her name. They'd know there was something phony about it, whatever he said. He must have paid someone to take her—someone pretty unscrupulous."

"I'm sure that's what he's done," Clare said. "He knows so many horrible people he wouldn't have had any difficulty. Oh, Lena, I'm so frightened . . . !"

Suddenly, all the pent-up agony of the day exploded in a fit of uncontrollable weeping. She buried her head against Lena, her body convulsed with heartbroken sobs. Lena did her best to soothe her. Hugh stood by, his face pale with anger and distress.

When the storm had passed and Clare, from sheer exhaustion, had stopped crying, Lena said gently, "Well, now, let's be practical. We can't do anything ourselves about bringing Christine back because we don't know where she is, so there's only one thing for it, Clare—you'll have to see a lawyer, and the sooner the better. The question is, who . . .?"

"I know a chap," Hugh said. "I met him on holiday last year with his family. He's a nice type—looks the perfect lawyer, actually, but he's very human. I don't think you'd find him difficult to talk to, Clare. His name's Harker."

He looked hopefully at Clare, but she said nothing. She seemed drained of vitality.

"I'll ring him at his home now, if you like. I'll tell him it's urgent—he'll probably see you in the morning."

"Lawyers always take so long about everything," she said.

"Well, that's all the more reason for seeing one right away."

Clare appeared so reluctant that at last Lena said,

"What else can you do?"

"I can go back to Arnold, I suppose," Clare said miserably.

There was a short, tense silence. Then Lena said:

"After what's happened? That would be pretty frightful hell, wouldn't it?"

"It's going to be hell anyway."

"Yes, but . . ."

"Oh, I know it would be humiliating to go back," Clare said, "and I should loathe every minute of it—but I should have Christine and I should know she was all right. It's so awful without her, Lena, and I'm so worried—I just don't think I can face it." Her voice was touched with hysteria.

"It's blackmail!" Hugh exclaimed. "Sheer blackmail!"

"Quiet, Hugh!" Lena said. "Now look, Clare, this is your own affair, and nobody wants to influence you against your own judgment, but do you honestly think it would work? You'd be completely in his power for ever after."

"Perhaps I could talk some sense into him. Perhaps in the end he'd realise it wasn't any good, and let me go."

"Do you really believe that? I don't."

"Perhaps I could go back for a short time," Clare said, "and then take her away again and make sure he couldn't get her. . . ."

"How? The man's a menace—he'll stop at nothing to get his own way. Besides, you can't play shuttlecock with the child, it isn't fair. . . . Listen, Clare, I know you've had a ghastly day and you must be absolutely worn out, but I do think you've got to be tough over this, for Christine's sake as well as your own. You should have legal advice, and get some proper arrangement made that's satisfactory for you and that Arnold can't wriggle out of, even if it does mean waiting. Don't you agree, Hugh?"

Hugh gave a troubled nod.

"In any case," Lena added, "there can't be any harm in making an appointment with Hugh's man. If you feel in the morning that you don't want to go on with it, you can always call it off."

Clare looked from one to the other of them. Lena's air of smart sophistication had deserted her—she looked motherly and worried. Hugh, his hands deep in his pockets, lounged uneasily against the mantelpiece, his eyes not leaving Clare's face. There was no mistaking their genuine concern for her.

"Well, make the appointment, then," she said wearily. "I'm just too tired to think any more."

Hugh took his hands from his pockets and went across to the telephone. Lena said. "What you're going to have, Clare, is a hot drink and a sleeping-pill."

If anything, the situation seemed even worse to Clare when she woke in the morning. The sight of the empty cot in the corner brought all her anxieties flooding back. The sense of loss was sharper. The prospect of remaining without Christine was unbearable. If she drove straight up to Hampstead now, she told herself, she would probably be able to catch Arnold before he left for the office, and they could arrange everything right away. The possibility that she might have Christine back in a matter of hours made the temptation almost irresistible. But when she thought of the price she must pay in hateful intimacy and utter submission, her body and mind rebelled and she doubted if she could go through with that, either. . . .Perhaps she should at least hear what Mr. Harker had to say first. It wasn't as though Christine was in any real danger—a day or so would make no difference to anything, and the decision to go back to Arnold would be open to her at any time. If the lawyer wasn't able to help, she could go back that evening, or the next day. . . .But she was still hesitating at breakfast, and it was only Lena's firm counsel that finally tipped the balance.

The appointment was for ten-thirty. At ten, Clare took a bus to the Strand, and then a slow lift to the sixth floor of a building opposite the Law Courts where the firm of Harker & Peabody had their offices. A young girl showed her into a waiting-room lined with dusty law books and pictures of famous judges, and she sat there for ten or fifteen minutes, nervous and impatient. Then the girl came back and said that Mr. Harker would see her.

Mr. Harker was a very tall man of forty or so, with glasses and a slight stoop and a precise but considerate manner. He shook hands, and drew out a chair for her opposite the window, and seated himself behind a desk with his back to the light. Clare, unable to restrain herself, said desperately, "My husband has taken my baby—I do hope you can get her back for me quickly." Mr. Harker nodded, and said that he'd understood as much from their mutual friend Mr. Cameron and that this kind of thing did occur quite often and they'd have to see what they could do about it.

Then, quietly and unhurriedly, he began to ask questions. It seemed extraordinary to Clare that he should want to know so much when the whole situation was as plain and straightforward as it could be, and all that was necessary was speedy action. Of course, she realised, he didn't know the first thing about her, but even so he was terribly inquisitive. There were probing questions about her marriage, about her relationship with Arnold, about why she'd decided to leave him. Questions, some of them, that seemed to invite denunciation of Arnold, which she was reluctant to voice to a stranger. She began to feel uncomfortable and embarrassed. It wasn't easy, without humiliation, to explain to another person just how one's love for a man could change in a comparatively short time into active dislike—particularly when some of the most vital facts couldn't even be mentioned. Clare did her best, but Mr. Harker sounded puzzled. Was there any other man, he asked, apologetically but firmly. Was she sure there wasn't? In that case, had there been any cruelty? Any mental unkindness? When had she first been aware of the change in her feelings? Had there been some precipitating cause that had brought about her departure from the matrimonial home? Any judge would want to know that.
. . .

She was beginning to hesitate over her answers now, and she suddenly realised why Mr. Harker had placed her opposite the window. She could scarcely see his face at all, but he could see hers. Gently, he pressed her. Unless she was absolutely frank with him, he said, it was unlikely that he would be able to help her. Naturally, everything she said would be treated in the strictest confidence. . . .She must try to regard him as she would her doctor.

In the end she overcame her reticence and told him about Arnold's illegal business deal, and about Mr. Chappell, and how Arnold had dismissed the whole thing as unimportant, and how she'd suddenly felt that she couldn't stand any more; and Mr. Harker seemed relieved, as though her story had begun to make sense to him at last. But now there were more complications, because he seemed to think that for her own sake she ought perhaps to disclose these things, and she had to tell him she wouldn't say anything that might be the means of getting Arnold into serious trouble—not, she added, if there was any other way of recovering Christine. . . .

Mr. Harker let the point pass, and put more questions. What were her long-term wishes about Arnold?—as though she cared whether she had a divorce or a legal separation or nothing, while Christine was still missing! Had she warned her husband that she intended to leave him, before actually doing so? Had she told him where she intended to go? Where *had* she gone? What was her financial position? Was there any possibility that she might some day want to return to her husband? Was he fond of the child, or had he taken it solely to bring pressure on her? Was he very much in love with her . . . .?

A little pause then and at last some advice. Mr. Harker was strongly against her going back to Arnold, merely to get the child. It would be a false basis, the marriage would be a mockery, it could never work. . . . Well, she knew that!

"But what *am* I to do?" she cried.

Still no definite reply, still the agonising caution, as Mr. Harker probed and considered! A suggestion, finally, that perhaps as a first step he himself should write to Arnold and try to reason with him. *Reason with him*!

"He says that possession is nine points of the law," Clare said bitterly. "He doesn't *want* to be reasonable—he wants *me*. It would be an utter waste of time."

"I see. . . ." Soothing words, now, from Mr. Harker—a sedative for a fractious child. "Well, we shall find some way, never fear. . . ."

But what way?—and when?

"He's stolen my baby and hidden her," Clare said, tears of frustration in her eyes. "Surely something can be done—*quickly?*"

More explanations, in a carefully detached voice. It was very doubtful whether a parent could steal his own child. Personally, Mr. Harker didn't think he could. The father and mother were both the natural guardians of their children, and with regard to guardians—here Mr. Harker quoted, not without relish, from some archaic text—"if one taketh the infant out of the possession of the other, the other hath no remedy by action of law but to take the infant out of the other when he sees his time."

Shuttlecock!

However, Mr. Harker went on to explain, the Court could interfere in the interests of the child—and there was always a strong presumption, a *very* strong presumption, that a child of tender years should be in the custody of the mother in the event of complete separation. There were difficult and unusual features about this case, but—well, perhaps they should consider a custody action. ...Mr. Harker spoke the last words with evident reluctance, as though he felt he was being forced prematurely into an opinion by beauty in distress.

What would be the prospects in a custody action, Clare asked, and how long would it all take? *How long?*

Now Mr. Harker was back at the beginning again—thinking aloud, it seemed. The judge might well want to know more than Clare was prepared to tell. It would hardly be enough for her just to say that she didn't like her husband. Of course, a good deal would depend upon the judge. ...And once the case was put up to the higher authorities, they would obviously have to come to some decision ... As to how long it would take, well, in these matters one had to be patient.

Patient!

"I should like to give a little more thought to the matter," Mr. Harker said finally. "What I suggest, Mrs. Hunter, is that you come and see me again on Monday morning, say at eleven. By then I may be able to give you more definite advice."

Clare looked at him with an expression of hopelessness. Monday was a year away! She knew now that her instinct about lawyers had been right. To Mr. Harker, hers was just one more case. It didn't matter to *him* how long it took. *He* wasn't being tortured. ...And Hugh had said he was understanding!

Mr. Harker came round from behind the desk. As she prepared to leave, he put a hand on her shoulder—a surprisingly firm hand, but gentle. "It may seem that the law moves slowly," he said, "but if the freedom and rights of the individual are to be protected, that's unavoidable. ...One thing's quite certain—your husband won't be allowed to get away with this. Sooner or later you'll have your baby back, without sacrificing yourself, so try not to take things too much to heart. I realise very well what you must be going through just now, but—well, life's not over yet."

She felt ashamed of herself then, because she'd given way to self-pity, which was what Arnold did, and because she knew she'd been unfair.

"Thank you," she said.

She didn't go back to Arnold during the week-end. The temptation remained, but with Mr. Harker's assurances in her mind, and Lena and Hugh bolstering her up, and her own natural courage to some extent restored, it seemed better to hang on for a day or two. And when, on the Monday morning, she saw the lawyer again, his attitude was so much more positive, so much brisker, that he carried her along with him. He was now in favour of starting an action at once to give Clare sole custody of the child. As far as her reasons for leaving Arnold were concerned, he thought they could make the harsh dismissal of an old employee the culminating point in a story of progressive disillusionment. With a persuasive counsel to represent her, he said, and a bit of luck over the judge, there was little doubt that she would be successful.

"In fact," said Mr. Harker, "on reflection I really can't see that your husband will be in a position to defend this action. If he does, he'll be inviting questions on his general behaviour, including—for all he knows—his reasons for getting rid of Mr. Chappell, and he'll scarcely want to risk having that brought up. Then again, he can hardly claim that the child is better off with strangers than she would be with you, and if he admits that he's simply using the infant as a means of coercion it's as good as saying that he doesn't care about her interests and he's bound to forfeit all sympathy. His best course would be to hand the child back and come to a sensible arrangement without going to trial, and I'm sure his own lawyer will advise him in that sense."

Clare sighed. It was so difficult for anyone to understand Arnold who didn't actually know him. "I doubt if he'll consult his lawyer," she said. "He seems to consider himself above the law. He's got Christine, and I think he'll just ignore everything we do and go his own way."

"H'm . . ." Mr. Harker pondered. After a moment he said, "I'm just wondering if there's any danger that he might try to send the child abroad. That would make things very difficult for us."

Alarm spread over Clare's face. "I don't know where he'd send her, but he might—especially when he knows that we're trying to get her back. I think he's in the mood to do anything."

"In that case," said Mr. Harker, "perhaps we'd better apply for an injunction to prevent him sending her outside the jurisdiction. . . .We shall ask for her to be made a ward of court when the action comes up, of course, and if we succeed, that will give the necessary protection—but in the meantime I think an injunction would be a wise precaution. We shall need your affidavit in support, and I'll have that drawn up at once. . . ."

Clare nodded. Now that she had placed herself in the lawyer's hands, he had only to say what he wanted of her. . . .But one question, the old question, still nagged at her.

"How long is it all going to take?" she asked. "When will I get her back?"

"I can only tell you," Mr. Harker said, "that I will give the matter my constant and personal attention, and that we won't waste a single day."

There was no difficulty about obtaining the injunction, but there was some difficulty about serving the various notices on Arnold, because he was out of town during the early part of the week and once again he had not told his office where he could be found. But he was back before anyone had time to get really agitated over the problem, and on the Thursday evening Mr. Harker was able to telephone Clare and tell her that the notices had been served.

Now came the hardest part of all—the long wait before the hearing of the action. Mr. Harker had done everything in his power to have it set down for an early date, but even so a delay of several weeks seemed unavoidable. For Clare, they were weeks of desolation. It was quite impossible, she found, to adjust herself to life without Christine, even temporarily. Through every moment of every day she was conscious of the awful void, the ache that was worse than a physical pain because there was nothing she could do to relieve it. Night after night she lay awake, wondering and worrying. Not knowing was the worst part—not being able to visualise where Christine was, or how she was, or what she was doing. There were moments when she felt that she simply *had* to go and see Arnold and appeal to him again—though her reason told her that she might as well appeal to a brick wall. There were moments of such desperate longing that she was tempted, even now, to abandon the whole action and surrender herself and her independence to get Christine back. But the days passed, and somehow she continued to exist, and not to weaken. She exchanged long letters with her parents in Singapore, she went mechanically through her professional engagements, she kept in close touch with her lawyer, and for companionship she leaned heavily on Lena and on Hugh. Lena had insisted that until things were cleared up she should stay on at the flat, and she had been very thankful to do so. When the others were around, she made an effort to conceal her misery and as far as possible avoided talking about her situation, since there was nothing new to say.

Then, at last, the call came from Mr. Harker. On a fine morning towards the middle of July, Clare dressed carefully in an attractive but demure suit and took a taxi to the lawyer's office and accompanied him across the Strand for the hearing of the action. She felt extremely nervous, but Mr. Harker seemed to think that wasn't at all a bad thing. He said he was certain she would make a good impression and assured her she had nothing to worry about. Arnold had entered no defence, and he didn't think the judge would have any difficulty in making up his mind.

The case was heard by a Judge in Chambers, and the atmosphere was much less formal and intimidating than Clare had expected. The judge was not even robed. He was a little, spare man, in an ordinary dark suit, and he looked at Clare in quite a friendly way from behind his desk. The only touch of legal panoply in the small office room was the wig and gown of young Mr. Forbes, her counsel. Clare was not required to give evidence herself, because once more she had sworn an affidavit. Mr. Forbes put the situation briefly and succinctly, laying emphasis on the fact that Arnold was using Christine as a lever and had no real concern for her welfare. The judge asked one or two questions, and then said without hesitation that he couldn't imagine an infant of such tender years would be better off anywhere than with the mother, and made an order giving Clare sole custody. Arnold was to hand Christine over to her at the flat at eleven o'clock on the following Monday morning, and notice would be served on him accordingly.

Clare was still not inclined to take anything for granted, but Mr. Harker assured her that High Court orders were rarely disobeyed, and once the notice had been served on Arnold it was clear that he'd ceased to worry. In the end, his confidence infected her, too. There were only a few preparations to be made for Christine's return, but they helped to pass the interminable week-end and she lingered over them lovingly. She made up the cot with fresh linen, and set up the playpen, and spread out Christine's favourite toys with the teddy bear in a conspicuous place. She filled the room with flowers, and afterwards sat there for a while, living the longed-for moment in imagination. She wondered if Christine would still remember her after all these weeks, whether she'd have changed at all, whether she'd have cut any more teeth. . . .

It was impossible to settle to anything. Sunday was a day of mounting expectancy, like the Christmas Eve of a child. A long,

38

wakeful night followed. Then it was Monday, and there were only a few more hours to go. Lena went off at nine, telling Clare to ring her as soon as she could and give her all the news. At ten, Mrs. Teeling arrived. She had already been told what was happening, and was almost as excited as Clare herself. At ten-forty-five Mr. Harker drove up in a taxi, and Mrs. Teeling brought coffee into the sitting-room.

At five to eleven another taxi turned into the mews. For a moment Clare's heart beat wildly—but it was a stranger who got out, a neighbour's bell that was rung. She continued to wait tensely by the window. Eleven o'clock struck—and now she couldn't contain herself any longer and walked to the end of the mews to keep watch from there. Cars came by frequently, but none was Arnold's. Slowly, the minutes passed. At eleven-fifteen he still hadn't come. She told herself that the traffic must be bad, that even a court order couldn't prevent a man being held up in a block. . . .

Suddenly she heard the telephone ringing in the flat. She raced back indoors—it could be Arnold, to explain the delay. But it was only Hugh seeking news. She told him there wasn't any, and talked to him for a moment or two, and then joined Mr. Harker again. It was nearly half-past eleven. The lawyer's face was grave, and Clare knew that it was futile to expect Arnold any longer. He had never intended to come. Probably the court order was just another piece of red tape to him. She should have known. In her heart, she *had* known.

Events moved quickly after that. Mr. Harker had devoted all his working years to the service of the law, and he hated to see it flouted. Also, he had developed a genuine sympathy and liking for Clare. It was therefore a very determined man who took her back to the Law Courts to apply for what he called "a writ of attachment" and a bench warrant for the arrest of Arnold. Clare felt a mere cipher as the machinery of the law turned dramatically—"We . . . command you to attach George Arnold Hunter . . . to have him before us touching the contempt . . ."

But by now the whereabouts of Arnold had become obscure,

and the court tipstaff, seeking to execute the warrant, was unable to find him. Apparently he had not put in an appearance at the office that day, and although his car was at Hampstead, he was not. The law, it seemed to Clare, was always a little behind him and, what was worse, gave warning of its approach. Arnold had obviously had plenty of time to make his arrangements and slip off quietly while he was still safe.

Even Mr. Harker looked dejected when he parted from Clare that afternoon. He had done his best for her, done all that any lawyer could have done, but the thought didn't give him much satisfaction.

"I'm afraid," he said, "that your husband is a very reckless as well as a very stubborn man."

She scarcely troubled to nod. She had been trying to tell him that from the beginning.

"What will they do now?" she asked.

"Well, the police will take over from this point. They'll circulate his description—they have a very efficient routine in these matters. Probably they'll notify the ports."

"He may have left the country already."

"We must hope not, Mrs. Hunter."

"What will happen if they find him?"

"When they find him," said Mr. Harker grimly, "he will go to prison until he has purged his contempt. That will mean, in this case, until he apologises for his conduct and produces the child. We have had a setback, Mrs. Hunter, but I really don't think that you have any reason to despair."

That evening, shortly after six o'clock, two police officers called on Clare at the flat. A heavily-built man with a spade-shaped jowl and shrewd eyes introduced himself as Detective-Inspector Raikes, and his companion as Detective-Sergeant Hawkins, and explained that they'd come about her husband.

"Do you mean you've found him?" Clare said, with sudden hope.

"Not yet, ma'am. We've only just begun to look."

"Oh! I thought for a moment you had news."

40

"Perhaps you can help us, Mrs. Hunter. We wondered if you'd mind accompanying us to your house in Hampstead. We need to know what your husband was wearing when he left there, and you can probably tell us which of his clothes are missing."

Clare hesitated—but only for a second. It wasn't going to be pleasant joining in the hunt for Arnold, with prison waiting for him at the end of it, but she couldn't afford to be squeamish. "Yes, of course," she said. "I'll come right away." She scribbled a note for Lena, and quickly joined the inspector in the back seat of the police car.

The journey didn't take long. Raikes, who had evidently briefed himself well on the case, asked Clare a number of pertinent questions which she did her best to answer, and then they were at the house and the two men were following her inside.

"While you're checking up on the clothes, Mrs. Hunter," Raikes said, "perhaps you'll allow us to have a look round, too?"

"Do anything you want to," she said.

She went into the downstairs cloakroom and glanced at the pegs. Arnold's light grey overcoat was missing; so was his soft grey hat. Upstairs, she found that he'd taken not only his grey pin-striped suit, but also a dark one. Two pairs of shoes had gone, as well as slippers, dressing-gown, and a pile of shirts and underclothes. In fact, she soon realised, he must have packed a considerable part of his wardrobe into the two large suitcases that had disappeared from the top shelf. Wherever he was, it looked as though he intended to stay away for some time.

She returned to the sitting-room to report, but the detectives were still busy. She could hear them rummaging about in various rooms, opening drawers and cupboards, obviously making a very thorough search. It meant nothing to her—the house was a house of ghosts and she had no feeling for it any more. The room in which she sat was dusty and neglected, and she realised that Mrs. Dodds must have stopped coming. Arnold wouldn't have wanted her around, of course, while he was preparing to leave.

It was nearly half an hour before the inspector reappeared. He had a cabinet photograph of Arnold in his hand.

"Could you tell me, Mrs. Hunter, if this is a fairly recent picture of your husband?"

She glanced at it, and nodded. "Do you want it?"

"We'd like to borrow it, if you don't mind. . . .By the way, did your husband have a passport?"

"Yes—he kept it in the bureau in his study."

"H'm!—well, it's not there now, I'm afraid. . . ."

Raikes saw the sudden look of fear on her face, and added, "I shouldn't worry too much about it, though—it could be just a precaution. In any case it doesn't mean he's taken the child abroad—that would be quite a difficult job, believe me. . . ." He sat down on the settee and took out his notebook, "Now what about these clothes? . . ."

Clare told him what she had discovered, and he wrote down the details. At the end he gave an approving nod. "Well, that should help us quite a bit," he said.

He looked up as Hawkins appeared in the doorway. The sergeant had an envelope in one hand and a piece of paper in the other, and he was holding them gingerly by their corners.

Raikes said, "Something interesting, Sergeant?"

"I think so, sir." Hawkins laid his finds carefully on the table, and Clare and the inspector bent over them. The envelope—a stamped one, the sort that post offices sell across the counter—was addressed in pencilled block letters to Mr. A. HUNTER at the Hampstead house, and was postmarked Wolverhampton. The paper was a mere scrap torn from a cheap pocket-book. A pencilled message on it, also in block letters, read:

MISTER HUNTER. SORRY TO REPORT THERE'S DISCONTENT BROKEN OUT. THE CUT'S OKAY WITH ME BUT LUCY'S GIVING TROUBLE AND THE MISSUS RECKONS THERE'S NOT ENOUGH IN THE DEAL TO MAKE IT WORTH WHILE. SHE SAYS TO TELL YOU SHE WON'T GO ON WITH IT IF YOU DON'T PAY MORE SO WHAT ABOUT SOME EXTRA DOUGH TO SWEETEN THINGS? SAY WOLVERHAMPTON TUESDAY? A.

There was a short silence while they studied it. Then Raikes said, "Nice work, Sergeant. Where did you find it?"

"In the pocket of an old raincoat, sir—on the back of the cloakroom door."

"Careless of him!" said Raikes, "Well, it looks as though we may be on to something."

Clare, very pale, said, "It *must* be to do with Christine."

"It certainly sounds like it," Raikes agreed.

"It couldn't be anything else—look at the date on the postmark. June 17th. Arnold took Christine on June 16th. It's absolutely right."

"H'm!—it didn't take them long to want more money, did it … ? What did your husband do on the 16th—was he away the whole day?"

"From eleven in the morning till about seven in the evening."

The inspector considered. "Yes—he could just about have done Wolverhampton and back."

"He *was* away on the following Tuesday, too," Clare said. "I remember, because my lawyer was trying to serve a notice on him and couldn't find him."

Raikes nodded. "Well, that all seems pretty conclusive. . . .Have you ever heard him talk about Wolverhampton, Mrs. Hunter? Any friends or business connections there?"

"Not that I know of—I don't think he ever mentioned the place. But there were a lot of things he didn't tell me about."

"I don't suppose this initial, 'A,' suggests anyone in particular?"

She shook her head.

"Do you know of any woman called Lucy?"

"No."

"H'm! The message doesn't give much away, does it …?" Raikes read it through again, frowning.

Hawkins said, "If 'A' and Lucy and the missus were getting a 'cut,' sir, presumably someone else was getting one, too. I wonder what *they* did to earn it?"

"That's a point," said Raikes. He was still staring at the message. "You know, the wording strikes me as a bit odd at the end, here.

If 'A' was actually living in Wolverhampton, he'd hardly have written 'Say Wolverhampton Tuesday,' would he?"

"Maybe he lives a few miles outside it, sir," Hawkins said.

"Maybe, Sergeant. . . .But that would mean the rendezvous wasn't at his own house, so you'd think he'd have mentioned a place and a time. Wolverhampton's quite a large city, you know."

"Perhaps there was a pub or something where they'd met before," Hawkins suggested.

Raikes grunted. "Well, we'd better ask the Wolverhampton people to make some inquiries—they'll find the trail pretty cold by now, but they may be lucky. . . ."

"Shall we take these things along to the lab., sir?"

"Yes, and let's hope we find some prints—if 'A's' the type he sounds like he may be in the records. . . .Ready, Mrs. Hunter?"

Clare had been copying down the message, so that she could show it to Hugh and Lena. "Yes, I'm ready," she said, after a quick check. "You'll let me know if you find out anything, won't you, Inspector?"

"I will indeed," Raikes said.

For the next thirty-six hours, Clare see-sawed violently between hope and the blackest depression. No further word came from the inspector, but on the following day the evening newspapers—which had made only the barest mention of the case so far—printed Arnold's photograph over helpful and almost identical captions, which at least showed that the police had started on the publicity job. Clare still felt very worried about Arnold's missing passport and the possibility that Christine might already be out of the country, though the pencilled message seemed to offer some slight reassurance over that. As Hugh pointed out, if Arnold had really managed to place Christine with a family in Wolverhampton, that seemed to make it less likely that he would since have gone to the trouble and risk of taking her abroad. What Clare couldn't get out of her mind for a second was the horrifying mental picture the message had conjured up—of three rough and grasping people, concealing Christine for money in some squalid Midland tenement.

She had a modelling appointment at Hugh's studio in the morning, but she found it almost impossible to keep her thoughts on what she was doing. Hugh didn't appear to be concentrating as he usually did, either—he was going through the motions of posing and lighting, but that was about all. And suddenly she knew why.

"Hugh," she said accusingly, "you don't intend to use these pictures, do you?"

He looked embarrassed, but she pressed him, and finally he had to admit it. "I'm sorry, Clare," he said, "I didn't want to upset you, but it's no good—we'll just have to wait until this business is over. You look as though you didn't have a wink last night, and it shows in spite of the make-up."

"I know," she said. "Oh, Hugh, what *am* I going to do?"

He gave her a pat on the shoulder. "Cheer up, old thing," he said, "it can't last for ever."

"My money won't last for ever, either."

"Well, you don't have to worry about that," he said briskly. "We can always have a whip round! Come on—I'll buy you a drink."

Early next day a reporter rang up from one of the newspapers to ask if he might call and see Clare, and when a car drew up in the mews shortly after eleven she thought it must be he. But it wasn't—it was Inspector Raikes.

"Morning, Mrs. Hunter," he said. "May I come in?—I've got news for you."

"Have you found her?" she asked eagerly.

"Not yet—but we've found your husband . . . He was picked up at Holyhead last night, trying to cross to Ireland."

"To Ireland!" At once, all Clare's fears came surging back. "What about Christine?"

"I gather he refused to talk about her, Mrs. Hunter, but I don't think you've any fresh cause for anxiety. Judging by his movements lately, it seems most unlikely she's been sent abroad. . . ." Raikes followed Clare into the sitting-room. "Apparently he's been staying for the past two or three days at a place called Llangollen in Wales."

Clare looked at him blankly. "Llangollen . . .?" she repeated.

"Yes, he travelled from there to Holyhead by local trains yesterday afternoon—gave up a single ticket. That's how we knew he'd been there. Does Llangollen mean anything to you at all?"

"Nothing ... I've heard the name, of course—but not from Arnold."

Raikes nodded. "Well, it's a holiday place, mainly—but your husband would scarcely have been taking a holiday with a warrant hanging over his head. In fact, it must have been extremely important business that kept him there, because if he'd left twenty-four hours earlier he'd have got out of the country without difficulty. He won't say what the business was, either. It seems a pretty fair bet that it was something to do with your daughter."

Clare, completely bewildered, said, "But why Llangollen? Surely that's miles from Wolverhampton?"

"It is, but then it's a long while since that message was sent from Wolverhampton—by now the child could easily have been taken to Llangollen. ...This is pure speculation, of course, but I did wonder if perhaps the Wolverhampton people had been a sort of first shift, with another lot of people in Wales taking her over later. That would account for each party getting a 'cut'."

"Yes, I see. ...But what could Arnold have been doing there that was so important? Not just visiting Christine, I'm sure."

"Well, if the luggage he had with him is anything to go by, he intended to stay in Ireland for some time, so it's quite possible he had to make some new arrangements before he left. ...But, again, that's only guesswork."

"Will the police be making inquiries at Llangollen?"

"They will if it's necessary, but now that we've found your husband I don't expect it will be. The fact that he wouldn't talk last night is nothing to go by—he's not likely to keep it up. We ought to get the whole story from him pretty soon."

"What's happening about him?" Clare asked.

"The tipstaff's gone up to fetch him—they should be down here by to-morrow morning."

"Shall I be able to see him?"

"Oh, yes, I imagine so. In fact, I think you should. I'll get in touch with you again, Mrs. Hunter, as soon as I know what arrangements are being made."

"Thank you," Clare said.

As things turned out, though, she didn't see Arnold. When Inspector Raikes called next day it was to tell her that her husband was not only maintaining his silence about Christine but was refusing to meet her and discuss the matter. Instead, he had sent a letter.

It read:

My dear Clare,

I trust you have been enjoying yourself during our long separation. I won't pretend that my plans have gone exactly as I intended—I'd have preferred to watch developments from Ireland and points beyond, rather than from a cell in Wormwood Scrubs, where I seem to be bound as a result of your stubbornness. However, I think you'll agree that I'm still in command of the situation as far as you and I are concerned. My original offer still holds good—all you have to do is to promise to live with me again as my wife, and you shall have Christine at once. Otherwise, I'm afraid it will be a very long time before you see her. Nobody is going to force me to give her back to you against my will. I don't suppose I shall take kindly to prison life, but then I don't suppose you'll take kindly to being without Christine indefinitely. It will be interesting to see who cracks first.

Ever your
Arnold.

That afternoon Clare went to see Mr. Harker again and took the letter with her. He read it through carefully, an expression of mounting distaste on his face. But he didn't seem particularly dismayed.

"Well, Mrs. Hunter," he said finally, "if you should ever wish to divorce your husband on grounds of cruelty, I should imagine that this letter might be quite helpful. In the meantime, I really don't think that you should take it too seriously."

"But he sounds so certain of himself," Clare said.

"Naturally he'd want to give you that impression, but he may well be bluffing. Even if he isn't, he won't be able to keep it up. He may seem full of fight at the moment, but prison life will soon change that."

"Do you think so?"

"I'm sure of it. Prisons are very dreary places, you know, especially for an intelligent man—dreary, and degrading. The loss of freedom, the tedium, the discipline—these things soon become insupportable for any man who isn't obliged to put up with them. Particularly, I'd say, for a man like your husband, who so obviously expects to have his own way in everything."

"But people *have* stayed in prison when they didn't have to," Clare said.

"They've usually had a very powerful reason. If a man is extremely fond of his child, he'll put up with almost anything in order not to lose it. If it's a matter of conscience—religious conscience, for instance—he'll sometimes defy the courts for a long time. But I've certainly never heard of anyone voluntarily staying in prison out of spite—not for long, anyway. The motive isn't strong enough."

"If he still hopes I'll go back to him," Clare said, "isn't that strong enough?"

"He'll soon come to realise there's no possibility of that—and then his attitude will change. My guess is that in a week or two at the outside, and perhaps in a few days, he'll decide that the game isn't worth the candle, and then you'll hear from him again. . . ."

Clare sighed. "I wish I had your confidence," she said.

A week passed—a week of almost no developments. Inspector Raikes called once more, quite early on, to ask if Clare had a recent picture of her daughter which he could usefully circulate to the newspapers, but the only ones she had were some that Hugh had taken when Christine was four months old, and to anyone but a mother the baby would have looked very much like any other baby at that age.

The police had not, Raikes admitted, made any appreciable progress in their efforts to trace Christine. The Wolverhampton inquiries had so far yielded nothing. The only fingerprints on the message from "A" to Arnold had been too blurred to be of any use. At Llangollen it had been established that Arnold had stayed for two nights and two days at a hotel called the Swan and had hired a self-drive car from a local garage while he was there—but so far no one had been able to discover where he had driven to. Clare had the impression that the police shared Mr. Harker's view that Arnold would talk very soon, and so save them the trouble of further investigation. Indeed, according to the inspector's information, he was already showing signs of restiveness in prison. Clare had replied to Arnold's letter, on Mr. Harker's advice, saying firmly that she would never allow herself to be coerced, but she was finding the war of nerves an almost intolerable strain and she knew that if something didn't happen very soon she would have to give way.

Then something did happen. On the morning of the tenth day she had word from the prison that Arnold was asking to see her urgently, and that it would be convenient if she could go along at three.

Meeting him again, across the gulf of anger and resentment that had divided them for weeks, was an ordeal—and a shock. It hadn't occurred to Clare that he would have altered greatly, and she was appalled at his appearance. Prison, the bitterness of defeat—something, anyway—had changed him beyond belief. There was no complacent smile now, no trace of the cocksureness that had been so marked in his letter. His eyes, as he glared at her across the table, were full of hatred; malice froze his face like a paralytic stroke.

"So you've come for the surrender!" he said. "You must be feeling very pleased with yourself. Ten days, and you win a complete victory—that's what you're thinking, isn't it? Quite a triumph!"

She shook her head. "I'm not pleased with myself. ...I'm just—terribly anxious and worried."

"Well, you're not the only one," he said. "I've got some news for you. ...Last night a couple of nosy parkers came to see me and questioned me about my business affairs. Do you know why? Because that swine Peebles has told them I was mixed up in the aluminium deal. So now I'm for it."

"Oh, Arnold . . ."

"*Oh, Arnold. . .*" he mimicked. "Is that all you've got to say?"

"What can I say? Only that I'm very sorry."

"*Sorry* . . . Why, if you hadn't left me the way you did, I'd never have been in this jam—I'd have been out of the country before they could touch me. It's entirely your fault. As it is, I shall probably get seven years. ...That surprises you, doesn't it?—but then you don't know everything, not by a long chalk. There's no harm in telling you now that there were some other little matters I kept quiet about—a lot of purchase tax I didn't pay, for one thing. And then there was a signature. ...They're looking into all that, now. They're going through the books. They'll find out all there is to find—and there's plenty . . . So now, you see, I shall have to stay in prison whether I want to or not. I've nothing to lose any more. Funny, isn't it?"

"Arnold . . ." Clare gazed at him in sudden terror. "Arnold, where's Christine?"

He shook his head, watching her, savouring every moment. "You got me into this, and by God you're going to suffer for it. You wouldn't come back to me, would you? You didn't care what happened to me as long as you were all right? Well, now you're going to pay. If I've got to rot in jail, you can rot, too. I'm not going to tell you where Christine is. You can forget her." Clare gave a little gasping cry, and the warder looked across at them sharply and Arnold dropped his voice to a venomous whisper.

"You shouldn't have treated me the way you did—you shouldn't have left me. That was something I couldn't stand—something I'll never forgive. All the time I'm in prison I'll be sustained by the thought that you're going through hell, too. Don't imagine that I'll ever want to forgo that pleasure. Don't imagine there's any way out for you. Before I set off for Ireland I made long-term arrangements. The people who've got Christine are being paid in a way you'll never discover, and the money won't run out. They've taken her over for good. From now on, she's their child. They'll give her a new name. They'll bring her up their way. They'll teach her to talk their language and behave the way they behave. She'll probably grow up a little slut. And you'll never see her again—your precious Christine. *Never!*"

He pushed his chair back and nodded to the warder. "I'm through," he said. "You can take me away."

Chapter Three

"Well, one thing's quite clear," Lena said, "it's no good looking for a change of heart from that psychopath." It was the evening of the same day, and she and Hugh had just been told about the prison visit. "We can write him off. Now the police will simply *have* to find Christine."

Clare nodded. She looked strained and tense, her eyes dark-circled in the pallid oval of her face, but she had herself well under control. Her first reaction to Arnold's vicious outburst had been shock—a dazed numbness, as though a landmine had exploded near her—and on the telephone to Inspector Raikes immediately afterwards she had been barely coherent. But the succession of hard knocks she had taken over the past few weeks had toughened her a lot, and the sense of shock had soon passed, and her thoughts had become wholly practical. She felt almost relieved that the choice of returning to Arnold had been taken from her—that, now, there was only one course for her to follow.

Hugh, still a little shaken, said, "What *is* the latest news from the inspector?"

"Well, there's nothing very definite, yet," Clare said, "but he's hoping that the money angle may produce something. He seems to think that if the people who've got Christine are being paid regularly, it may be possible to trace the payments in spite of what Arnold said. Anyway, he's going to work on it."

"What about the Llangollen inquiries?"

"He's leaving those to the local police for the moment. He wasn't exactly encouraging, but he did say we might get news at any time."

Hugh chewed on his pipe. "It seems extraordinary to me that we haven't had something already," he said, "either from there or from Wolverhampton. Surely it can't be all that easy to hide someone else's child."

"Evidently it is!" Clare said.

"Well, I don't understand it. . . .How can you prevent other people knowing when you've suddenly brought a new baby to a house? Even Christine yells sometimes—and there'd be clothes to hang out, and special shopping to do, wouldn't there?—all that sort of thing?"

"Perhaps they're not trying to prevent other people knowing," Clare said. "It isn't as though anyone's going to recognise her."

"They'd have to have a darned good explanation ready for neighbours and tradesmen and people, all the same—who she was and where she'd come from and how they'd got her—and that wouldn't be exactly simple to work out. I'd have thought they were running a pretty big risk, myself."

"They could say they were looking after her for a relative," Clare said. "Lots of people do that—for a short time, anyway."

Lena frowned. "You know," she said after a moment, "I rather agree with Hugh—I wouldn't imagine they'd feel very happy about it. After all, presumably the police are making inquiries about babies that have suddenly appeared from nowhere, and there's been quite a bit about the case in the papers by now. Suppose *you* lived in Wolverhampton, or Llangollen, and you read somewhere that a stolen baby was believed to have been brought into the district, and you knew that a baby of the right age had just arrived next door and that it didn't belong to anyone there and you discovered that no one ever seemed to visit it—wouldn't you start wondering? It *would* be a risk. And don't forget that these people are helping Arnold to defy a court order, now—if they were found out I should think they could get into pretty serious trouble themselves."

"I suppose Arnold's paying them so well that they're willing to take the risk," Clare said.

"But the pay would stop if Christine were found—and that

would worry them, even if the legal side didn't. They'd want to feel very sure they weren't going to be discovered—and I certainly wouldn't feel safe in their position, especially if I were living among people who knew me well and who'd never heard about any baby in the family before ... In fact, I wouldn't be happy until I'd got away to some new place where I wasn't known, and could start all over again as though the child were mine. Then it would be quite different."

"That's the obvious way," Clare agreed.

Hugh suddenly leaned forward in his chair. "I say, you don't suppose that's what's happened, do you?"

Clare said: "What do you mean, Hugh?"

"Well, up to now we've been taking it for granted that there were two lots of people concerned in the affair—one at Wolverhampton and one at Llangollen—but we could be wrong about that. Perhaps there's only one lot. They could have been living in the Wolverhampton district when they first got Christine, and then they could have moved out and gone to Llangollen—just as Lena says. It could all have been part of the plan—all fixed up in advance."

"If there aren't two lots of people," Clare said, "how could the money have been shared? Aren't you forgetting that message?"

"Oh, yes—of course." Hugh was silent for a moment. "Still, we don't know that the second 'cut' was for looking after Christine, do we? Couldn't someone have done some minor job, and been paid for it?"

"What sort of job?"

"Well—making arrangements, looking for a suitable house—transport, perhaps—there must have been an awful lot to do. We've no definite evidence that it was Arnold who took Christine up to Wolverhampton in the first place—all we know is that he wasn't around that day. He might have got someone else to do it. That would make sense of the message, wouldn't it?"

"I suppose it would," Clare said.

"It seems much more likely to me—something of that sort, anyway. After all, would Arnold really have wanted to involve two separate families in the job of looking after Christine?—even if he'd been able to, which wouldn't have been easy. It strikes me as so cumbersome and unnecessary, and it would certainly have doubled the risk. . . .What do you think, Lena?"

"I agree," Lena said. "I think the idea of one family making a move is far more likely. But not, surely, to Llangollen?"

"Why not Llangollen?" Clare asked.

"Well, for one thing, because of that message again. It had a sort of cockney ring in my ears—towny, anyway. Tough, urban types, I picture them as. I can't see people like that going and burying themselves in the Welsh hills. In fact, I doubt if they'd be able to—they'd stick out like sore thumbs. If they planned to make a move so that they could start all over again, the obvious place to go to would be some big city like Birmingham or Manchester, where neighbours wouldn't be so curious and they could lose themselves in the mass. . . .How big is Llangollen?"

Hugh said: "Got an A B C.?"

"Over there on the bookshelf."

He was back with it in a moment, flicking over the pages. "Here we are," he said. "Llangollen, Denbighshire. Population, 3,275."

Lena nodded. "You see what I mean—it's not much more than a big village. And you know what villages are like for gossip."

"But Arnold hired a car, don't forget," Clare said, "and there are quite a lot of biggish towns close by. There's Wrexham and Whitchurch and Oswestry—I was looking at the map before you came in. Shrewsbury's not very far away, either."

Hugh turned the pages again. "Shrewsbury—population, 44,926."

"Well, that's a bit more like it," Lena agreed. "All the same, if I'd been looking for a snug hideout I'd still have preferred Birmingham. What would have been the point of going to a small town?"

"There may have been some good reason we don't know about," Hugh said. "Perhaps this chap 'A' had heard of some special job that would suit him—how can we possibly tell? What we do know is that Arnold went to Llangollen and stayed there for two days, and it's a thousand to one his visit had something to do with

Christine, so it's no good our saying it's not a likely place—we've just got to accept it, at least as a starting point . . . Of course, there may be absolutely nothing in this moving idea, but it does seem to make quite a bit of sense—and if there *is* anything in it, there's a chance that Christine might be traced quite quickly. After all, even in a biggish town there can't be all that number of people moving house at the same time."

"You mean the police might do a street-by-street inquiry in all the towns within a certain radius?" Lena said.

"Something like that. We could put it up to them, anyway."

"Well, if they took that on they'd need someone around to help them—someone who knew Christine. It wouldn't be much good checking up on people who'd just moved into the district with a baby if they didn't know whether the baby was the right one or not when they saw her."

There was a moment's silence. Then Clare said: "Do you think I ought to go up there?"

Lena regarded her thoughtfully. "Perhaps you ought . . . At least you'd be on tap if they wanted you."

"I don't know why I didn't think of it before. Of course—it's idiotic for me to stay down here when I'm one of the few people who would recognise Christine right away. Even if I only drove around, it would be something. Why, I might even *see* her!"

"With three people to look after her," Lena said, "I shouldn't think they'd risk taking her out much."

"They might. They might get careless and not bother. Anyway, I'm sure I ought to be there. Don't you think so, Hugh?"

"It's a pretty long shot . . ." Hugh said.

"I know it is, I've no illusions about that—but what else have I to do? It's quite hopeless for me to try to work—I look a hag, and my mind's not on it. And I can't just sit here and wait."

"You'll find it very lonely up there on your own."

"I don't care—I've *got* to do something. Even if I don't do any good, I'll be happier searching than just twiddling my thumbs."

"Well, you're probably right about that," Hugh said. Lena nodded.

"Then that's settled." Clare was all eagerness now. "I'll drive up there to-morrow."

"I'd come with you if I could get away," Lena said, "but I don't think there's a hope—not this week."

"Shall *I* come?" Hugh said. "If you're really planning to comb the district, four eyes are better than two."

"Hugh—*could* you?"

"I don't see why not—I'll have to do a bit of phoning in the morning, that's all. I could manage a few days, anyway."

"But that would be a tremendous help—we could take both cars, we could cover twice the ground. . . .And I can't tell you how glad I'd be to have you."

Hugh looked at his watch. "In that case," he said, "perhaps I'd better go and pack."

Before they left next morning, Clare rang up Inspector Raikes and told him what she proposed to do. He seemed doubtful whether her trip would achieve very much, but he readily agreed that it couldn't do any harm and said he would get in touch with the Denbighshire police and let them know she was coming.

Hugh turned up in his rather elderly Ford around ten, complete with camera and sketch book and a stack of ordnance survey maps that he'd bought on his way to the flat. By eleven they were driving out of London along A.5. It was a warm and inviting day, and the August traffic was heavy, but the thought of Llangollen, the thought that every mile was taking her nearer Christine, gave Clare an unaccustomed impatience on the road. In her new, fast car she was able to nip in and out among slow convoys where Hugh was constantly baulked, and soon, without intending to, she had left him well behind. But they joined up at lunchtime for a picnic by the roadside, and again near the Wrekin for tea, and by the early evening, dusty and tired after their long, hot drive, they were running together into Llangollen.

It was, they discovered, a rather pleasant little town, with a superb setting. It lay in a broad sheltered valley between wild hills, with the picturesque river Dee running through the centre of it, and a fine promenade beside the plunging water, and an ancient bridge with irregular arches that made Hugh's fingers itch for a pencil. Most of the big hotels—including The Swan, where Arnold had stayed—had attractive positions overlooking the river and were already crammed with holiday-makers. Hugh and Clare had some difficulty in finding rooms, and it was with relief that they finally managed to get fixed up in a modest pub called The Anglers on the bank of a canal.

Immediately after dinner they walked round to the police station and introduced themselves. The station sergeant had had a message from headquarters and was expecting them, but he explained that the officer in charge of the inquiries about Christine, an inspector named Ellis Jones, had been busy that day on another case and wouldn't be available until the following morning. Could they come back at eleven o'clock next day? They said they could, and thanked him, and set off for their next objective, The Swan.

On the way, they had a look round the town—and it didn't take them very long. The place managed to give an impression of enormous activity, with its stream of holiday cars still winding through on A.5, its bunches of tourists taking the evening air, its little knots of people on the bridge, its cafés and restaurants and milk bars, and its shops displaying knick-knacks and trinkets—but it was actually quite tiny. As Lena had said, it was scarcely conceivable that anyone would have planned to hide a baby in this, or any comparable, place. The larger towns, or the lonely, isolated hills—these, surely, were the alternatives? It seemed most unlikely that Llangollen could have had any interest for Arnold except as a convenient centre to drive out from. And even that raised problems.

"I wonder what he'd have done," Hugh said with a slightly puzzled air, "if he hadn't been able to hire a self-drive car when he got here? Bit of a risk, I'd have thought, in a small place like this—particularly in the height of the season."

"Well, he must have been pretty sure about it," Clare said, "or he'd have come up in his own car. He could have left it in a garage here just as well as at home. Perhaps he fixed it all up beforehand by phone."

"It's something we might check up on," Hugh said.

They had reached The Swan, now, and after a word with the girl at the reception desk they were shown into the office. The manager was very friendly and understanding when Clare explained who she was, but he had already told the police all he knew about Arnold Hunter, which was very little. Mr. Hunter, he said, had rung up from London on a Thursday and reserved a small single room which happened to be free. He had arrived on the following Sunday—the day, Clare recalled, before the Monday when he should have been handing over Christine. During his brief visit he had spent almost all his time out of the hotel. On both days he had gone off soon after breakfast, taking a packed lunch with him, and had not been seen again until after six. Each evening he had retired to his room immediately after dinner, apparently without talking to anyone. He had had no callers, and he had received no messages. As far as the hotel was concerned, his visit had been entirely uneventful.

Clare asked if she might look at the register, and the manager had it brought in for her. She soon found Arnold's signature—a bold "G. Arnold Hunter," with the usual self-conscious flourishes. She glanced at the names above and below it, but they meant nothing to her.

She was rather thoughtful as they strolled back towards The Anglers. "You know," she said presently, "I'm a bit surprised that he registered in his own name. If Christine is really in the district, I'd have thought that he'd have tried to hide the fact that he'd been here. But it seems as though he wasn't bothering at all."

"He couldn't hide his face," said Hugh, "so why trouble about a signature? He must have known there'd be photographs in the papers once he disobeyed the court order."

"That's true, but it isn't always easy to recognise people from newspaper photographs, particularly if you've only had casual glimpses of them. A name's different—especially a name like 'G. Arnold Hunter.' It seems such an unnecessary risk, when he could just as well have signed himself 'George Smith.'"

"Well, it's a point," Hugh agreed, "though I don't know where it gets us."

"There's another thing," Clare said. "In all the time I've known Arnold, I can't ever remember him eating a packed lunch. He loathed the idea of picnics—if he was out and wanted lunch he always went to the best hotel he could find. It's really very odd. . . ."

Inspector Ellis Jones was waiting for them in his office when, sharp at eleven next day, they returned to the police station. He was a tall, dark, pale-skinned Celt, with a drooping black moustache that gave his face a slightly mournful appearance. Tiny drops of perspiration glistened on his forehead, as though he had already been active in the morning heat. He greeted them politely, but with a noticeable absence of enthusiasm, and it soon became apparent that he didn't think they were going to get anywhere as a result of their visit to Llangollen.

"Before you can begin to search, Mrs. Hunter," he said, his voice rising and falling in a soft Welsh lilt, "you need to have some notion where you intend to look, and at present you have no notion at all. Of course, there is always the chance of a miracle, and if you were prepared to search for weeks and months all round the district you might by pure chance happen to see your baby, and we should be very glad. But I think that what we have done is more likely to produce results."

"What have you done?" Clare asked.

"Well, for one thing we have instructed all our officers to keep their eyes open as they go about their duties and report anything unusual that concerns a baby. Then we have had inquiries made about the car your husband was driving, in the hope that someone may have noticed where he went to. Unfortunately it was a little grey Austin, a very popular type of car, and all our roads are full because of the holidays, hundreds an hour we get through Llangollen itself, and picnickers all over the place. So it is difficult, but perhaps someone will remember seeing him somewhere, because of all the photographs there have been in the papers. And if we receive any information we will act upon it at once, you can be sure of that. . . ." He mopped his forehead, and began to fiddle with a paper on his desk.

"Yes, I see," Clare said. She was thinking that it was more than a fortnight since Arnold had been at Llangollen—that it was unlikely anyone would recall him at this stage, if they hadn't done so already. After a moment she said, "There was one thing that occurred to us which we thought might help. . . ." Briefly she explained Hugh's idea that the people who had Christine might recently have moved into the district.

The inspector followed her with close attention—but at the end he shook his head. "It's an interesting idea, Mrs. Hunter, and of course you may be right—but to act on such a theory would involve us in a long and difficult inquiry. There are so many towns in the district. There is Chester, with fifty thousand people, and Shrewsbury with forty thousand, and many other smaller places besides, so where should we begin? Naturally, we want to find your baby, but we are very short-handed here and other forces are in the same position and it is not, after all, as though the child is in grave danger. In the circumstances I do not think we should be justified in mobilising large numbers of men for such an unpromising search. I am sorry."

Clare looked rather hopelessly at Hugh, who so far had been quietly listening and pondering. Now he took over.

"I wanted to ask you about the car, Inspector. Do you happen to know if Mr. Hunter booked it before he got here?"

"No, he didn't," Ellis Jones said, "he just called in at the garage on the Monday morning to see what could be done, and he was very nearly unlucky. At first he was told there was no self-drive car available, but I understand he was very pressing, see, and said he would pay anything he was asked, and in the end some arrangement was made so that the people who had booked the car used a taxi instead for those two days and Mr. Hunter had the self-drive car."

Hugh frowned. Arnold, of course, had always acted on the principle that money would get him anything he wanted. . . . But it still seemed an extraordinary chance to have taken.

"What explanation did he give for all the fuss, Inspector?"

"Urgent business, he said, and not liking to be driven by others. A very self-willed man, he was!"

61

"And didn't he drop any hint at all about where he was going or where he'd been?—not even the direction?"

"Not a word."

"What about petrol? Did he have to fill up anywhere on the road?"

"Unfortunately not, Mr. Cameron—there was enough in his tank to last him."

"Do you know how many miles he covered?"

"Yes, I can tell you that, because he had to pay according to the mileage. He did seventy-two miles."

"I see. . . . Did he take the car out on both the days he was here?"

"He did, yes. He kept it in the car park at The Swan, and the porter says it was away both days, from morning until evening."

Hugh nodded, and was silent for a moment. Then he said: "Look, Inspector, this is just an idea and there may be nothing in it—but if he went somewhere on both days, isn't it quite likely that he went to the same place twice, and that he didn't go anywhere else? After all, he'd have been most anxious to get to Holyhead—he wouldn't have been in the mood for sightseeing."

"It's possible," Ellis Jones conceded. "Just possible."

"Well, if he did go to the same place twice, and nowhere else, he'd have done thirty-six miles each day—eighteen there, and eighteen back. That would rule out Chester and Shrewsbury and all the other large towns, wouldn't it? So a thorough search for newcomers to the district might be much easier than you think."

"Do you mean, Mr. Cameron, that we should draw a ring round Llangollen at eighteen miles, and inquire at all the houses near that radius?"

"Would that be a very big job?"

"It would be a much bigger job, I am afraid, than the situation justifies. I am speaking now from the public point of view, you understand. If we were investigating a murder, or some other serious crime, it would be a different matter entirely—then any reasonable theory would be worth following up, however long it took. But in the existing circumstances . . ." He shook his head.

"At least," Clare said, looking at Hugh, "it might be something for us to work on."

The inspector gave a faint shrug. "By all means, Mrs. Hunter, if you have the time to spare. But my own opinion is that you are much more likely to find your baby as a result of information received. That is what almost always happens, you know—someone notices something unusual and comes to us—or perhaps there are quarrels and someone talks ... In any case, I feel sure we shall have news for you before very long, from one source or another. And now, if you'll excuse me. ..."

He got up, and shook hands, and a moment later they were being politely shown out.

"*I* don't believe they're even trying," Clare burst out indignantly, as they walked away.

Hugh gave a non-committal grunt. "They're certainly not breaking their backs over it—though I suppose it's understandable enough, if they're short of chaps."

"I don't see what could be more important than a stolen baby," Clare said.

"She's top priority for us, old thing, but she isn't for them and we've just got to face it. They obviously think she'll turn up—in fact, I wouldn't be surprised if they still thought Arnold would come clean in the end."

"Then it's a good thing we came here, that's all I can say. Just imagine if we'd stayed in London, waiting and waiting, and nothing at all had happened ... At least we've got a definite job to do now."

"You mean the eighteen-mile idea?"

"Why, yes—I thought it was brilliant."

"It could be very misleading," he said. "Arnold would only have had to go back to his hotel by a slightly longer route on one of those days, just for a change, and the calculation would be right out. ... And, of course, we don't *know* that he went to the same place twice."

"If he was up here to see people about Christine," Clare said,

"I should think it's almost certain. Look, Hugh—if he'd finished his business the first day, he'd have gone straight off to Holyhead, wouldn't he? As he didn't, it obviously wasn't finished—and in that case he'd have gone to see them again."

Hugh nodded. "That's how I worked it out—but what business could have occupied him all that time?"

"There must have been a lot to discuss. Perhaps they had more trouble over money?"

"Heavens, they could surely have come to terms in a day. . . ." Hugh looked at her eager face, and added, "Still I agree we've no other basis to work on at the moment. We'd better get the maps out and see what we're up against. . . ."

There were four inch-to-the-mile sheets covering the area, and marking the eighteen-mile points on them proved to be a long and laborious job. Hugh used a piece of string, measuring out from Llangollen along one road after another and making a little cross at the end of each eighteen inches. Once away from the town, there were dozens of different routes to be reckoned with, many of them minor roads and some no more than tracks. A lot of them petered out among close mountain contours before the eighteen-mile point was reached, and that helped, but there was still an embarrassment of choice. Hugh worked on the assumption that Arnold would have gone to his destination by the shortest route, and when, as sometimes happened, there was doubt, the alternative was included. They had to break off for lunch, but by three the task was finished, and all four sheets were clearly marked with a big, irregular circle of crosses.

"I suppose," said Hugh, a trifle wistfully, "we ought to take different sectors and join up again in the evening."

"Why, yes, Hugh, of course."

"All right—you take the western bit, and I'll do the north." He gave her one of the maps. "Shops and garages will probably be the best bet, when you can find any handy—they ought to know if someone has just moved into the district . . . I suggest we aim to get back here around six thirty."

Clare nodded. She went quickly across to her car, and a moment later she was driving away with a look of concentration on her face. She was as keen, Hugh thought sadly, as though she were off on a hot scent.

They saw little of each other during the next day or two. They met briefly at breakfast, and again at dinner and for an hour or so afterwards, when they exchanged reports on their activities and planned their routes for the next day before taking themselves wearily off to bed. Hugh, though he was applying himself to the search with the utmost vigour, somehow always managed to get back to the pub before Clare did, and always found that she had covered the greater mileage. Now that she had something positive to do, nothing would stop her, apparently, but sheer exhaustion. She seemed to have become hypnotised by the figure "18," and Hugh wondered uneasily what would happen when there were no more places to visit and almost wished he'd never had the idea about the eighteen miles in the first place. But he consoled himself with the thought that, for the moment, at least, she was too busy to mope.

Their experiences on the job proved to be very similar. Sometimes the marked points occurred close to villages, and then the inquiries were comparatively easy to make. Sometimes the cross on the map coincided with some isolated dwelling, and then they allowed themselves to be affected by atmosphere and their hopes rose. Sometimes they found themselves in a waste of open country at the eighteen-mile spot, and then there was nothing to ask about. They both had the same tussle with steep mountain roads and hairpin bends; the same problem of finding their way among confusing moorland tracks; the same difficulty about establishing friendly contact at remote farms where the people were often reserved and suspicious, and the dogs barked menacingly. Neither of them met with the least success, except in a negative way. Wherever they went, the local folk were quite sure that if any "foreigner" *had* just moved into the neighbourhood with a small baby, they would have known about it. It soon became apparent to both of them that what Lena had said about the "sore thumb" applied even more to the countryside than it did to the small towns, and that it would have been quite impossible for "A" and his wife and Lucy to have settled down anywhere in the district without drawing some attention to themselves. But having once started on the eighteen-mile theory, it seemed only sensible to go on to the end and make quite sure.

They were now roughly half-way round the circuit. On the morning of the third day, Hugh switched to the eastern sector and Clare to the southern. She found it easier going, here, for the hills were lower, the network of roads was closer, and there were more habitations in the valleys. Quite often she was able to cover two or three of the marked points with a single inquiry. The answers were still consistently negative and she was working quickly round the arc when suddenly, at about three in the afternoon, she was brought up sharp with the very piece of news she had been hoping all along to hear. A woman who kept a shop in a tiny hamlet said that some strangers had just moved into a cottage not far away and that they had a small baby, a girl.

Eagerly, Clare sought more facts. How old was the baby, she asked, and what was it like? About fifteen months, the woman thought—very dark and pretty. Clare's heart beat faster. Were there three people, she asked, as well as the baby? No, there were only two—just a man and his wife. "Oh!" Clare said. That was a set-back—though perhaps it wasn't conclusive. Lucy, after all, could easily have been left behind. When had they moved in, she asked, and where from? From the Midlands, the woman said, about four weeks ago. The wife, she added, was Welsh, but the man was English. He'd come into the district to take up a job with the local quarry company. She hadn't seen anything of the man, and couldn't say what he was like. The wife was on the quiet side, and so far the pair hadn't mixed very much with anybody. . . .

It took Clare only a few minutes to find the cottage, a low stone structure called Tan-y-Bryn, at the foot of a hill. There was washing hanging out at the back, some of it baby clothes. Clare rapped loudly on the door, but no one came. She tried to look inside, but the windows were small and the rooms dark and there was little to be seen. Presently she returned to the car, and settled down to wait, her thoughts in a turmoil. She scarcely dared to hope—yet there were so many things that seemed to fit. The family had come from the right district, at the right time, and more or less to the right place. The cottage was about a mile from the nearest marked point, but Hugh could easily have made a small error in measuring winding roads on a map. If the wife was Welsh, that might be a reason for the man seeking a job in Wales. . . . Lena hadn't thought of that.

For over an hour, Clare waited in the car, her nerves stretched almost to breaking point. In imagination, she could *see* Christine here. . . . It wasn't impossible—it wasn't as though she hadn't worked for this. But she mustn't count on it—it would be idiotic to count on it. . . . Hope and doubt chased each other through her mind. If only they would come. . . . Then, just before five, she heard a hoot behind her, and an ancient single-decker bus came rumbling by and stopped at the cottage gate. A young woman got out, with a baby and a folding pram. She threw one sharp glance at the car and went quickly indoors before Clare could reach her or see the baby's face. Clare followed her up the path, sick with uncertainty. As she raised the knocker the door opened again and the woman said "Yes?" She had the baby in her arms—and it wasn't Christine.

For a moment Clare could scarcely speak. Then she said, in a shaky voice, "I'm sorry to trouble you—I wonder if you could let me have some water for my radiator?"

It was a heavy disappointment, but Clare refused to let it get her down and next day she continued with the search as doggedly as ever. By now, though, there was little more ground to cover. Around four in the afternoon the circuit was completed, and she and Hugh converged once more upon The Anglers. Hugh arrived first, dusty and dry after the usual fruitless questioning. Clare drove up ten minutes later.

"Any luck?" he asked, as he joined her at the car. She shook her head.

"Nor me," he said.

"Well, that's that, then, isn't it?"

He tried hard to think of something encouraging to say, but couldn't. "Look, what about a cuppa at the Waterside Café? I'm absolutely parched."

"Good idea," she said.

The Waterside Café (Prop. J. Sears) was an attractive little open-air restaurant adjoining a boatyard, about a couple of minutes' walk along the canal bank. There were a dozen tables dotted around a lawn under gay umbrellas, and they found a vacant one and dropped thankfully into wicker chairs. Hugh gave Clare a cigarette, and began to fill his pipe.

"Well, there's one thing about it," he said, "we must have made everyone baby-conscious for miles around."

"It's about all we have done," Clare said. The drug of action, even ineffective action, was already wearing off, leaving her with a visible hangover. "Where do we go from here, Hugh?"

"I'm blessed if I know. ...The trouble is, we've no lead at all now—only an idea that's flopped, and a lot of loose ends. ... I must say I'm beginning to have a bit more sympathy with that cautious inspector!"

Clare gave him an anxious glance. "You don't want to go back, do you?"

"Not unless you do."

"I certainly don't. ... After all, none of the basic things have changed. Arnold *was* here, and he *was* seeing people about Christine, I'm positive of that, and just because one theory hasn't worked out ..."

She broke off as an elderly, rubicund man approached with a tray. Judging by his air of genial independence, this was J. Sears in person. He looked at them closely for a moment, then gave an affable smile.

"Grand day! "he said. He had a robust Midland accent. "What can I get you?"

Clare said, "Just tea and scones, please." and turned again to Hugh. "I'm sure the truth can't be far away—the only question is, where are we going to look for it?"

"Well," Hugh said, "the eighteen-mile idea hasn't produced anything, but the moving-house idea may still be all right. I suggest we try a bit of prospecting farther afield—say, some of the larger market towns."

"It seems a pretty big proposition now, doesn't it?"

"It always did."

"I know, but the haystack looks bigger when you're near it."

"We could call on the house agents—that might cut the size down a bit. ... Even if we don't get anywhere, we'll be stirring up fresh interest all the time."

"That's true ..." Clare said.

By now, Mr. Sears had returned with the tea, and they sat back and watched him lay out the cups and plates. His manner was so amiable that their own silence seemed a discourtesy. After a moment, Hugh said, "This is a very pleasant spot you've found."

Mr. Sears nodded. "Grand, isn't it?"

"Have you had the place long?"

"Five years last May—but I'd had my eye on it for twenty years before that!"

"Really?"

"I had, that. I used to say to myself, 'Jim, lad, when you retire that's just the spot for a nice little café and boatyard'—and five years ago the dream came true." He emptied the tray, and gazed proudly over the smooth lawn and the peaceful water to the line of distant hills. "Finest place on the cut—and that's saying a lot."

"On the what?" Hugh said.

"On the cut. The canal."

"Oh—the canal. Yes, of course. ..."

Frowning, Hugh watched Mr. Sears move away to the next table. Then his gaze switched to the narrow ribbon of water that stretched away down the valley, and for a moment or two he was lost in his thoughts.

Suddenly he said: "Clare, I expect I'm being quite crazy, but could I have another look at that message—the one from Wolverhampton?"

"Of course." She put the teapot down and fished the crumpled copy from her bag and gave it to him.

"I've just had the wildest notion. . . ." He read the message through slowly. "Or have I . . . ? I wonder if we've been putting the wrong construction on this thing all the time?"

"What do you mean?"

"Well, this phrase THE CUT'S OKAY WITH ME . . . You don't suppose he could have been talking about a *canal*, do you?"

Clare stared at him. "Oh, Hugh, that's rather fantastic, isn't it?"

"Perhaps it is—but I don't know. . . . Here we are, looking for Christine in a place we're pretty sure she's been to, sitting beside a canal that's apparently called a cut, and the message says THE CUT'S OKAY—and after all, a canal is a route."

"But surely it's money he's talking about all through?"

"He certainly goes on to talk about money," Hugh agreed, "but the 'cut' part may not be about that. It's quite possible to read it another way—that the canal's okay with 'A' but Lucy doesn't like it and so the missus thinks they should get more pay. . . . Don't forget we were never quite happy about the idea of a 'cut' in the money sense, because there was no real evidence that anyone else had done anything to earn it."

"That's true." Clare bent over the message with new interest. "You mean that 'A' and his family may have gone to live on a canal?"

"They may work on a canal—judging by the tone of their message, it's just the sort of rough, tough job they easily could have. Families do, don't they?"

"Why, yes—they have long, narrow boats with cabins at the back. I've seen them unloading . . ." She broke off, suddenly tense. "Hugh!—I've seen them unloading *at Arnold's wharf!*"

Hugh gave her a startled glance. "Arnold's? I didn't know he had one."

"He has—his office is beside a canal. The Regent's Canal."

"Good lord!" Hugh said softly.

"So he'd know all about canals, he'd know boatmen."

"And a boat would be mobile—it could have come here without

70

attracting any special attention and they'd have had all the advantages of moving house without any of the problems. ...."

Fascinated, Hugh gazed again along the canal that had suddenly become so much more than a stretch of motionless, decorative water.

"I wonder if Wolverhampton's on a canal?" Clare said.

"That's a point. ... I'll go and get a map."

In a few moments he was back. They cleared a space on the table and spread the map out.

"Here we are," Hugh said, "Wolverhampton. Now, then—let's see. These are railways, these are roads—this dotted line must be some sort of boundary. ...What about these other lines?" His eyes leapt to the legend in the corner. ... "Why, Clare, it's a positive centre! There seem to be canals running in from all directions."

"Then things *are* beginning to fit," she said excitedly. "I've just thought of something eke. Do you remember how puzzled Raikes was about the phrase SAY WOLVERHAMPTON TUESDAY, because it didn't mention a time or a meeting place? Well, if 'A' was *living* on a barge, any time would have done, and as long as Arnold knew it was at Wolverhampton he could have found it quite easily wherever it was.... Hugh, I honestly believe we're on to something."

"Well, let's not go too fast," he said. He picked up the message again. "There are still some things that don't fit, you know. If this chap 'A' is a bargee, why should he say THE CUT'S OKAY WITH ME as though he'd just tried it for the first time—and for that matter, why shouldn't it be okay with his family?"

"Perhaps he meant that having Christine on the cut was okay with him, but not with them."

"He doesn't say that."

"Well, perhaps he's new to the job—they must take on fresh people sometimes. Perhaps Arnold told him to get the job."

"In that case, would he talk about the 'cut' in that familiar way?"

"He might—I shouldn't think it would take long to pick up the jargon. ... Anyway, there's something much more important than that. Does the canal at Wolverhampton join up with this one?"

Hugh followed the thin centipede line with his finger while Clare waited anxiously.

"Apparently it does," he said at last. "There's a junction at a place called Autherley—it becomes the Shropshire Union Canal there—and then there's another junction at a place called Hurleston, where it joins this one."

"There you are, then," Clare said, "it all fits perfectly. Arnold took Christine to a barge he knew about—it might even have been carrying some of his stuff. A day or two later he got this message to meet it at Wolverhampton, which he did. Afterwards, he kept in touch with its movements, and when he realised he'd have to leave the country or be arrested he fixed a rendezvous and met 'A' and his family up here to arrange things before he went. And he met them," she added triumphantly "eighteen miles down the canal! How's that?"

"It's quite a theory . . ." Hugh said.

"It's your theory, really, and I think it's a pretty good one. Why, it even takes care of the loose ends! Remember how odd we thought it that Arnold used his own name at the hotel? Well, if Christine was on a barge and he knew it was going to leave here almost immediately, he wouldn't have cared who found out that he'd been at Llangollen. In fact, it would have been a useful false scent."

"That's true," Hugh agreed. "Well, now—what are we going to do? Ask somebody about boats, I suppose."

Mr. Sears was collecting crockery from a table nearby. As he finished, and glanced across at them, Hugh beckoned him over.

"Do you get many barges up here?" he asked.

"Barges?" Mr. Sears savoured the word as though there were something unfamiliar about it. "You mean *working* boats. . . . ? Oh, no, we don't get any of those—there's nothing for them to come for. In the old days, now, this section was quite busy—used to be a good bit of coal carried up—but there's been no traffic of that sort since the war."

"Really?" For a moment Hugh looked quite nonplussed. Then he said, "Still, there'd be nothing to prevent one coming up if it wanted to, would there?—say to a place eighteen or twenty miles down the valley?"

"There'd be nothing to prevent it," said Mr. Sears, "but I can tell you there hasn't been one lately, if that's what's in your mind."

"Would you have known, necessarily?"

"I'd have known, all right. A working boat up here would be an event, see? There'd have been talk about it."

"Oh ..." Hugh could scarcely conceal his chagrin.

"If it's working boats you're interested in," Mr. Sears said, "you'll have to go to the Shropshire Union main line—Hurleston, Market Drayton, Autherley—that way. They're up and down there all the time. ...." He broke off as someone called for a bill. "Excuse me just a minute. ...."

Hugh looked at Clare. "Well, it didn't take long for that theory to hit a snag!" he said.

"I don't know—is it such a snag?" She was already beginning to adjust her ideas. "How far away from here is the Shropshire Union?"

Hugh consulted the map again. "It depends what part. Say thirty miles—perhaps a bit more."

"Well, couldn't the eighteen-mile point have been a sort of half-way house? Arnold might not have wanted to risk being seen near a boat—and 'A' could easily have taken a bus and met him somewhere."

"Yes, I suppose that's possible."

"Then the theory's still perfectly sound."

"H'm ... It's going to be much more difficult to test."

Mr. Sears was back, now, eager to pick up the threads of the conversation. "Yes," he said, "you'll find plenty of working boats on the Shroppie Cut."

Hugh said, "Do you know anything about them? The people who live on them, and where they go to—that sort of thing?"

"I ought to," said Mr. Sears. "I was in the business all my life till I settled here. Had a place in Birmingham—owned a whole string of boats at one time."

"Did you, though? Then perhaps you could help us ... ?"

"Half a minute," said Mr. Sears, "I'll just ask the wife to take over. . . ."

He was back almost at once. Hugh offered him a cigarette, and he drew up a chair and leaned forward with his arms on the table. "Now, then, what is it you want to know?"

"Well . . ." Hugh hesitated. "The fact is, this lady is looking for a baby—her baby. It's been—stolen."

Mr. Sears gave a sympathetic nod in Clare's direction.

"Yes, I heard about it," he said. "Llangollen's a small place."

"We wondered if it might have been taken on a canal boat."

"Ah! You mean you've reason to think so?"

"We've reason to think it's a possibility."

"Up this way, eh?"

"Yes. If we're right, the boat would probably have been travelling along the Shrophsire Union about two and a half weeks ago—but that's all we've got to go on. The thing is, how would we begin to trace it? There must be a lot of these boats."

"There are that—thousands of 'em, up and down the country. Still, a lot of them do short hauls and keep more or less on the same run."

"This boat would have been at Wolverhampton back in June. That was when the baby was taken."

Mr. Sears nodded. "Well, there's a pretty steady traffic between the Midlands and the ports—Ellesmere Port, Liverpool, Manchester. Most of the stuff on the Shroppie Cut's doing that run. To and fro, all the time. So if your boat was a regular, I'd say there was quite a chance it wouldn't be far away."

"Do you think anyone would notice if a boat had a new baby on board? Any of the other boat people, I mean?"

"I reckon they might. They all know each other, the canal folk do—they're like a big family. Those that have been at it for any length of time, that is. It'd get around, I dare say—and there's been plenty of time since June."

"What would be the best way to get in touch with them?" Hugh asked. "Are there special pubs they go to when they're on their runs?"

"Well, there are—but I don't know that you'd get much out of them that way. They're clannish, you see, they don't talk that easily to strangers. I reckon they'd be suspicious if you went into a pub and started trying to pump them—specially if you started talking about 'barges' . . . That'd put them right off. . . . No, what I always say is, if you want to make friends with people you've got to go in by the right door. Then you can talk to them casual-like."

"What *is* the right door?"

"Why, get on the cut. Take a boat and get in among them. That's what I'd do if I wanted information."

"Wouldn't it be just as good from the towpath?" Clare said.

Mr. Sears shook his head vigorously. "No one ever learned much about canals from the towpath. It's the old story—different elements don't mix. On the towpath, you're a landsman. Besides, what about the weather, what about grub—you might miss the very boat you wanted to see. Once you're *on* the water, you're there the whole time."

"But I'm afraid we don't know anything about boats," Clare said, with a glance at Hugh.

"Oh, you wouldn't need to worry about that—you'd soon learn. There's people go on the cut that have never been on water in their lives, and after an hour or two they're shooting the bridge holes and working the locks as though they'd been born to it."

"Working the locks. . . . ? Why, aren't there any lock-keepers?"

"There are, but they've other things to do—mending the towpaths, trimming hedges, looking out for leaks, all sorts of things. . . . You'd have no trouble, though—even young kids can work the locks. There's nothing in it."

"Well, I don't know. . . ." Clare said doubtfully. "Do *you* let out boats, Mr. Sears?"

"Only rowing-boats, lass—and you'd want a proper cabin boat. You wouldn't normally get one at this time of year, either, not without booking—I know there's none to be had on this section. But if you're interested I've a cousin over near Blampton who's got a boat—chap named Flint. He lets out two boats, as a matter of fact, sort of sideline he runs, and he's just had a cancellation for one of them. He was telling me on the phone this morning. Good boat, she is, nicely fitted out and easy to handle—you could walk aboard and be off in an hour."

"How far is Blampton?" Clare asked.

"Hour and a half's run. It's on the Trent and Mersey. You'd be back on the Shropshire Union in a couple of days, and after that you'd meet plenty of working boats and some of them would be pretty sure to know about the one you're after. . . .That's what I'd do, anyway."

The moment they were alone, Clare said eagerly, "What do you think, Hugh?"

"I think the old boy would quite like to get a client for his cousin's boat," Hugh said.

"Well, of course—but I don't believe it was just that. Was he talking sense, that's the point?"

"Oh, yes, I think so. About going in at the right door, anyway. The question is whether it's worth while going in at any door."

"If Christine *is* on a canal boat," Clare said, "and we were on one too, I do think there might be a chance of hearing something. . . ."

"*If* she is. . . .We haven't a single solid fact to build on, don't forget. The canal theory is fascinating, but it really is pretty thin."

"I know it is, Hugh—but so was the idea that started us searching in the hills for someone who'd just moved house, and that seemed worth while at the time, and we've much more to go on here."

"We'd be committing ourselves much more, too, if we took a boat. It still strikes me as a fairly ambitious undertaking for a couple of greenhorns, in spite of what Sears says."

"Oh, I expect we'd manage. . . .The thing is, Hugh, what else is there for us to do? Inquiring in the market towns wasn't going to be much more than a last resort, was it?—we'd really come to a full stop. . . . And if we did suddenly have a better idea while we were on the boat, we could always stop and follow it up. It isn't as though we'd be moving to some entirely different district."

"Well, that's true. . . ."

"Of course, I do realise it might mean your staying up here longer than you meant to. . . ."

"You don't know how long I meant to!" Hugh said with a faint grin. "After all, what's the good of being a free-lance if you can't take an extra week or two off when you need it?"

"Then you'll come?"

He gave a little shrug. "I'm game if you are. As you say, we shan't be losing anything—except, possibly, our lives! It's really up to you to decide."

"Then I think I'd like to try."

"In that case," said Hugh, getting up, "I'd better telephone Mr. Flint right away and tell him we'll be along in the morning."

Chapter Four

They checked out of The Anglers immediately after breakfast next day. Clare dropped a note in at the police station for Inspector Jones, telling him where he could get hold of her in case he should have news for her later on. Then they drove quickly across country in the two cars.

Blampton turned out to be a large village, pleasantly situated on the river Trent, but now almost submerged by the industrial sprawl from the Potteries. Mr. Flint had given Hugh detailed instructions how to get to his wharf, which they found beside a timber yard on an unsalubrious reach of the cut. He was waiting for them there—a short, active-looking man in his early forties. His face was prematurely creased with deep lines, but he had a ready and attractive grin and an engaging manner.

"Well, here's your boat," he said, pointing to her. "*Varley*, she's called—named after an 18th century canal engineer."

For a moment or two they gazed at the strange-looking craft without comment. She was strong but roughly built, thirty to forty feet long, and something over six feet wide. There was a small area of open deck at each end, but the rest of the space was taken up by a high, enclosed wooden structure with steeply-sloping sides and a narrow, flat roof. She looked exactly what she was—a box built on a boat's hull, like a Noah's ark—and aesthetically there was little to be said for her. A great curved tiller, apparently made out of iron piping, did nothing to improve her appearance. But when they stepped aboard at Mr. Flint's invitation—cautiously, because neither of them was used to the feel of a rocking boat underfoot—they discovered that everything inside was surprisingly comfortable. There were two cabins, one opening out of the other. They were light and airy, with big sliding windows and plenty of headroom. One had a bottled-gas stove and sink in it, as well as a deal table and chairs and a bunk; the other was smaller with two bunks. A tiny cupboard room off the second one had "all mod. con." Both cabins were fitted with electric light. Everything necessary for the trip—apart from stores—was already on board; linen, cutlery, crockery, utensils, maps and books. If Hugh liked to take the boat for a fortnight, Mr, Flint said, he could have her at a slightly reduced price.

Hugh looked at Clare, who was gazing dubiously at an object floating in the black, unsavoury water. "What about it, Clare. . . . ?" He followed her glance. "Surely you don't mind a dead rat or two?"

She gave a feeble smile. "I'd spend a fortnight on the Styx if I thought it would do any good. The boat's quite nice."

"All right," Hugh said to Mr. Flint, "we'll take her."

Mr. Flint looked pleased. "Then if you'd like to go and do your shopping I'll have her ready for you in about half an hour. You'll find you can get all you need in the village."

"Shall we be able to leave the cars here while we're away?"

"Yes, you can put them in that shed over there. It'll be locked up, so they'll be perfectly safe . . . By the way, which direction will you be going in?"

"We want to get to the Shropshire Union canal," Hugh told him.

"Well, either way will take you there. If you go to the right you'll have to pass through Stoke and the Potteries—they're extremely interesting, as a matter of fact, and the industrial part doesn't last too long. But there's nearly two miles of the Harecastle Tunnel—you tie up behind an electric tug for that. It's very noisy and water drips on your head all the time but it's quite an experience."

"I'm not sure I much like the sound of it," Clare said.

"Then I should go the other way—you'll find that very quiet and rural. You branch off at Haywood Junction along the Stafford and Worcester—the Stour Cut, they call it—and join the Shropshire

Union at Autherley. . . . Right, I'll make out your permit for Autherley, and get the boat turned round for you."

They nodded, and drove back into the village to do their shopping. While Hugh laid in groceries and beer in reckless quantities, Clare got herself a pair of slacks and a beret for the trip, and they both bought gum-boots. By the time they'd returned to the wharf, and unloaded, and garaged the cars, Mr. Flint had the boat freshly washed down and was ready to give them instruction. First he went carefully over the engine with them, explaining about oiling and greasing, and warning them to keep a close eye on the water-cooling system, and telling them how to clear the filter when it became choked with weed.

"If you get anything round the propeller," he said, "you'll probably be able to free it by going into reverse. Don't try to travel too fast—you'll only burn up your petrol, and if you make a wash along the banks you'll have the canal authorities after you. Always put the gear lever in neutral when you're approaching the banks, and shove off when you leave—there are lots of places where blocks of stone have fallen out of the embankment and you don't want to catch your propeller on them. Keep to your right when you meet other craft, but as near the centre of the channel as you can—canals are only about five feet deep in the middle, and very shallow at the sides, so it's easy to run aground. This boat draws about eighteen inches. . . ."

He touched the stern rope. "Always make sure this strap's coiled neatly inboard when you're on the move—if it gets round the propeller it'll mean an underwater job for one of you. . . ." Mr. Flint gave them a slightly sinister grin. "Now about the equipment . . ." He turned to the flat roof, where various implements were laid out. "You have a long shaft here, for pushing off when you get stuck, and a short shaft, and a gang-plank in case you can't get close in to the bank when you moor—you'll find that'll happen quite a bit on the Shropshire Union. . . . Two iron pins, and a hammer, for securing the straps when you tie up—you can stop pretty well anywhere, but try to avoid the outside of bends if there's likely to be any traffic about, because that's often where the deeper water is and you might be in the way. Oh, and if you're on a canal where there's any horse traffic, moor away from the towpath or you may get tangled up with the rope. . . ." He pointed to a set of tools that looked rather like car starting handles. "These are the windlasses for the locks. Different colours for different canals—green for this one. If you drop a windlass overboard it'll cost you fifteen shillings. Try to keep a clear run along the cabin top, or you may trip over something and take a header. . . . Now, if you're ready, I'll take you through the first lock and see you on your way. . . ."

Clare looked at Hugh. "Have you got that?" she said.

He grinned. "What do you think I am—an electronic brain?"

"How do you feel?"

"Scared to death!" He pressed the starter button, and with Mr. Flint's watchful eye upon him, slid the tall gear lever into forward and opened the throttle. *Varley* began to move purposefully away from the wharf.

"Tiller!" said Mr. Flint.

Hugh grabbed the tiller and pulled it hard over. Belatedly he realised that he had pulled it too hard and was heading straight for the opposite bank. There was a bump, and *Varley* stopped with a shudder.

"On a boat," Mr. Flint said, in a tone of gentle reproof, "sudden, violent movements should be avoided."

"Yes," said Hugh.

"Actually, you'll find this boat's quite a good swimmer."

"Yes," said Hugh—and stared. This, presumably, was a joke. "Well, it's nice to know she'll be able to save herself," he said.

"Just a canal term," Mr. Flint explained. "A boat's a good swimmer if she answers to her helm easily. . . ." He climbed up on to the cabin top and pushed *Varley's* head round with the shaft. "Now—try again."

Hugh manoeuvred the boat back into mid-stream and held her there, setting course for the first lock, which was already visible.

"You'll be going downhill as far as the Stafford and Worcester," Mr. Flint said improbably. "After that, you'll be climbing to Autherley.

". . . Better ease her down, now. Put her into reverse as you approach the lock gates and give the engine a burst and she'll stop quite quickly."

With a concentrated expression, Hugh steered the boat into the narrow entrance to the gates, which were closed, and brought her to a halt.

"Nice work! "said Mr. Flint. "All right, switch off now, and I'll tell you about the locks."

Hugh turned the engine off, and they all stepped ashore. For a moment Clare gazed down into the empty, cavernous lock. Its walls and gates were covered with a dark green slime, and were exposed to a depth of fourteen or fifteen feet. It looked most uninviting.

"I didn't realise they were so deep," she said, drawing back a little.

"Most of them are shallower than this—you certainly won't find any deeper ones." Mr. Flint peered into the hole with an appraising eye. "As a matter of fact, there's less water here than there should be. You'll probably find a paddle not properly closed at the next lock—that is, if you don't get stuck before you reach it. . . . Now, then have you any idea how locks work?"

"A vague idea," Hugh said.

"Well, it's all quite simple, of course—they're just a means of getting a boat up and down hill. A canal's divided into stretches between locks, called 'pounds'—which can be anything from a hundred yards to ten miles long. Around here, they're mostly short ones. Each pound is at a different level. You can see that the one the boat's in now is much higher than the one you're going into. Right! Now before you can get into the lock, you've got to have the water level there the same as the level you're on. That means that in this case you've got to fill it. The flow of water is controlled by things called 'paddles'—they're invisible sliding panels built into the gates. You draw them—that is, open them—by winding up the paddle bar with the windlass, and you drop them—close them—by lowering it First, though, you must make sure the bottom gates are shut and the paddles dropped there, or the water will simply run through. . . ."

For five gruelling minutes Hugh listened to Mr. Flint's technicalities. Clare made an effort to follow them, too, but with only moderate success. Still, the principle seemed clear.

"I suppose it's not really much more complicated than a camera, is it, Hugh?" she said hopefully, as Mr. Flint concluded his lecture.

"It sounds a damned sight more dangerous!" he said.

Now they both had to repeat in turn the basic points of the drill, the few essential movements, uphill and downhill, until they'd got them right. Then, at last, Hugh was allowed to draw the paddles, and they watched the lock fill.

"There's no point in trying to open the gates before you've made a level," Mr. Flint said, "because you won't be able to. Just stick your behind against the balance beam and put your weight on it, and you'll feel it move when it's ready. Don't face it and push it ahead of you, because if you slip you may crack your jaw!"

Soon the swirling water calmed down, the last eddies died away, leaving a still, foam-flecked surface. Hugh opened the gates, and Clare, nervous but determined, boarded *Varley* alone on Mr. Flint's instruction and started the engine and took her into the lock with only a slight bump or two. Hugh closed the gates behind her, dropped the paddles, and drew the paddles at the bottom gates. Slowly, the boat began to sink into the depths.

"If she starts rushing backwards or forwards," Mr. Flint called down cheerfully, "shove her into gear and give her a bit of engine. Watch out that she doesn't catch on any broken bricks as she goes down—if she does, rock her off. Some of the walls are in a bad state."

Clare looked apprehensively at the walls, but *Varley* still seemed to be going down. In a few minutes, Hugh was able to open the bottom gates, and Clare took the boat out, very gently, and stopped by the bank beyond, flushed with pride.

"Well, that's about all," said Mr. Flint, "You'll learn by your mistakes! Remember to keep the boat well away from the top gates when she's going down, or you may catch the stern on the sill—that's a ledge projecting below the gates—and find she's dangling in mid-air. I've known it happen, and it can mean very heavy repairs.

If you *do* get into trouble in a lock, drop all the paddles at once. And do make quite sure you leave the paddles properly shut behind you. If you don't, you may drain the pound you've just left and flood the one ahead of you, and that'll cost you a lot of money for wasted water. . . . Right, you're on your own, now. See you at Blampton in a fortnight. Good luck!" He grinned, and waved and set off back along the towpath to his wharf.

"My God!" said Hugh, staring after him, "no wonder his face is lined!"

For the first mile or two they handled the boat as circumspectly as though she were an unexploded bomb. Repeatedly Hugh peered over the side to check the cooling water, or threw nervous glances at the banks to make sure there was no wash, or mentally rehearsed the movements he would make if he had to stop the boat suddenly. Clare stood beside him on the afterdeck, her eyes intent on the channel ahead. *Varley's* maximum speed was no more than a brisk walking pace, but even at three miles an hour there were navigational hazards to be avoided—shallows on the inner sides of curves, protruding reed beds and tree roots, and patches of floating weed. Unfamiliarity gave a sharper edge to every imagined danger. The main steering problem came at the many bridges, which carried roads and tracks over the water. Here the canal always narrowed abruptly, as the towpath turned in under the arch, so that on each side there would be no more than a few inches to spare. Often, too, the bridges were on sharp curves, which made the approach even more difficult. Several times they cannoned off one side or the other as they crept slowly through, and twice they ran aground immediately beyond because they hadn't turned the boat's head quickly enough, and then Hugh had to go forward with the long shaft and pole off. But practice soon brought skill, and with no other traffic to bother them they were soon shooting the "bridge-holes" with assurance. They took turns at the tiller until they were both used to the feel of it—and it soon became apparent that Clare was the more reliable steersman. Hugh, fascinated by a whole new world of experience, had quickly abandoned his initial caution and was inclined to gaze about him, until a touch of the boat on the bottom brought him back to duty. Clare was single-minded about it, as she was single-minded about the whole enterprise, and gazed ahead with a fiercely-concentrated expression—"like Boadicea going into battle," Hugh said.

The locks, to begin with, were an exciting challenge, and they negotiated the first few with copybook care. There was usually an adjacent lock cottage, set in a profusion of flowers, but no one came out, no one took any notice of them, and they could spend as long as they wished in locking through. By the time they had stepped ashore, and reconnoitred the position, and filled the lock, and taken *Varley* in, and cleared floating branches and debris from behind the gates, and emptied the lock, and taken *Varley* out, and made sure the paddles were down behind them, it was quite normal for twenty minutes to have passed. But there was a lock at every mile or so, and each time it was easier, and soon they developed a smooth routine. Clare stayed with the boat, because the physical demands were less: Hugh climbed out and worked the paddle bars and gates. Clare had to face the leaks from badly-fitting gates that swamped the deck and sometimes threatened to inundate the cabin; she had to nerve herself afresh each time she sank into the dark depths. But Hugh had by far the heavier job, wrestling with groaning gates and dilapidated paddle posts and jammed cogs.

Gradually, as confidence came with experience, they began to take the locks in their stride, and even to look forward to them as stimulating interludes. It became clear to both of them that the cut, far from being the dangerous place they had first thought it, was in fact as safe as a sanctuary. Clare relaxed at last and started to take an interest in their surroundings. The canal, once a rough and ugly gash through the countryside, had long since merged with the landscape, and its pounds looked as natural as the reaches of the river Trent that meandered beside it. Everything seemed incredibly peaceful. Away to their left there was a busy main road, with week-end traffic grinding along nose-to-tail in the dust and smell and heat; but here on the water everything was tranquil, and they felt as remote from the rushing world as though they were travelling in a different dimension. Both Hugh and Clare had imagined canals to be straight and dull, but this one was neither. It wound continually, and each bend brought new and pleasant vistas, of trees and reeds and grassy banks, and cows grazing in the water meadows. Except for an occasional silent angler, the towpath was deserted. There were almost no houses. The few they saw by the banks were mostly crumbling, overgrown ruins, as though they'd belonged to the canal age and had died with it. Derelict barns and warehouses, designed in more gracious days for beauty as well as utility, still had an appeal for the eye. Stately homes, set deep in neglected parks, looked like something from *The Sleeping Beauty*. Everything to do with the canal had a forlorn and haunting quality. The creaking locks, the eroded banks, the ancient capstans worn by countless ropes to strange wine-bottle shapes, the bridge arches grooved and rasped by a century of towed traffic—all was touched with a melancholy yet attractive decay.

The hard work had made them hungry, and presently Clare cut sandwiches and opened a bottle of beer and they lunched at the tiller between locks without slowing their pace. Clare's one aim was to push on, to reach the Shropshire Union, and she was counting the locks and the miles they had put behind them like trophies. She had found a guide-book in the cabin, and an inch-to-the-mile map with the canal line thickened and the locks marked boldly, and from now on they were able to check their progress more easily. All through the warm afternoon they continued their descent of the Trent valley. From time to time they caught a delicious back-door glimpse of some tiny village, but for the most part the canal avoided inhabited places and there was nothing to mar the rural scene. Then, around six, they came suddenly upon Haywood Junction—so suddenly that they nearly missed the sharp right-hand turning into the Stour Cut. The guide-book talked of the junction as though it were a place of some importance, for it was here that the canal from the Severn met the Grand Trunk system from east to west; and they had expected signs of life. But all they found were some ivy-covered ruins, a dock choked with reeds, an abandoned toll office, and a picturesque bridge that carried the towpath in a single span over the mouth of the new canal. The junction was a joining of waters and a name on the map, and that was all.

If the Trent and Mersey had seemed deserted, the Stour Cut looked at first as though it might be unnavigable. Great beds of rushes and flags had eaten into the channel so that, looking ahead, it seemed to Clare that the way must be blocked. But *Varley* nosed slowly on, with plenty of depth under her hull, brushing aside the reeds, and after a while the channel opened out into a broad lake where the water was so clear that they could see the bottom. Moorhens scuttled away from their bows, and dignified swans convoyed them, and a heron took the air and wheeled gracefully past their stern. Beyond the lake they passed two men fishing from a square raft, but there was still no sign of moving traffic. Presently they began to look around for a suitable spot to moor, and chose a green bank on the towpath side and manoeuvred *Varley* in.

Hugh made the boat fast to the iron pins, and left Clare to prepare the supper while he went for a stroll along the path. His shoulders ached from the windlass work, and there were fat blisters on his palms, but he couldn't remember when he had felt more at peace with the world, and his conscience troubled him a little over that. It seemed callous that he couldn't share Clare's poignant anxiety all the time, that he was even enjoying himself. But she also, he thought, had had moments of diversion that day, if not of forgetfulness, and on all counts he felt glad that they had hired the boat. An appetising smell of cooking called him back to *Varley*. Anxious or not, Clare had managed to concoct a very acceptable meal from tins in a very short time and they ate with relish. By the time they'd finished supper, and washed up, and prepared the cabins for the night, dusk had fallen. For a few minutes they sat and smoked in the half-light, replete and drowsy.

"Quiet, isn't it?" Clare said.

"Wonderful! They can keep their space travel—I'll settle for this any time."

"I would, too, if I weren't in such a hurry."

"We haven't done badly, Clare. A dozen miles and almost as many locks—I'd say it was a good effort for a first day."

"We're about half-way, aren't we?"

"Just about. If we have an equally good trip tomorrow, we should be among the working boats by the evening."

"It can't be too soon for me." Clare said.

They were both up and hustling around soon after daybreak. While Clare tidied up the cabins and prepared breakfast, Hugh busied himself happily with the routine of the boat—greasing and oiling, pumping out the bilge, sluicing the roof and walls, washing the mud off the shafts, and making sure the propeller hadn't picked up any rope or wire. It was a beautiful morning to be out of doors—still and clear, with bright dew sparkling on the grass beside the towpath and the promise of another hot day. Hugh found it hard to believe that great industrial areas were all around them, for here on the cut not a soul, not a building was in sight. The only sounds were the hum of insects, the plop of fish, the clucking of water birds. He would gladly have lingered, but Clare was eager to be off and in fact he had *Varley* under way while she was still clearing the breakfast things.

The first mile or two took them very close to Stafford, and for a while there was a break in the rural scene. A large factory appeared on their right, and for nearly an hour they kept seeing it from different angles as the canal turned and twisted. Then they came on a stretch of viscid black water, with slag heaps close to the banks and the pit-head gear of coal-mines on the sky-line and an acrid chemical smell in the air. But it didn't last. Before long they were moving through green country again, with extensive marshes on their right and a rich bird life to watch. The canal wound continually, often turning right back on itself, with bends that called for all their steering skill. Bridges rose out of the fields in unlikely places, and often it was hard to tell whether they had already passed under them or had still to go through them. The cut remained narrow and weedy and completely deserted.

Presently they began to climb a series of locks that were very close together. Hugh was finding the lock work tougher than on the previous day, for on this semi-derelict canal many of the gates were rotten, their paddle bars rusted and their ratchets stiff. Some of the locks were so choked with weed and debris that he had to flush them out before Clare could take *Varley* in. Some had crumbling brickwork, sprouting coarse grass. Some had bottom gates which leaked so badly that it seemed the locks would never fill. Some had lock cottages that were empty, ruined shells. Everything spoke of neglect. But the countryside was attractive, and in spite of their condition the lonely locks, with their gracefully outspread beams, improved rather than spoiled the landscape.

Clare found that she liked the feeling of going up. As *Varley* glided slowly up to a pair of closed lock gates, the way seemed barred, and the end of the pound felt like the end of a journey. But once inside, the boat rose quickly and buoyantly, and all at once a new and exciting vista would open out—a deeply satisfying moment. Soon, though, the pounds became so short that one lock followed almost immediately upon another, and then there was little to see and it became a hard struggle to gain a few hundred yards. But they battled their way through, and came at last to a place called Gailey—shown on the canal map as Gailey Top. With no more locks ahead for many miles, they felt that they had reached the summit of the world and stopped for lunch with a pleasant sense of achievement.

The first part of the afternoon spell was restful. Clare took the tiller; Hugh had little to do but keep an eye on the cooling water, and bask in the sun, and admire the mellow brick bridges they were passing under, each with a number and each with its name inscribed on an ancient iron plaque. Then the scene changed again. The cut became very narrow and overgrown, so that they had to watch out for overhanging tree boughs that threatened to sweep everything off the roof top, and navigate with care. Along this narrow stretch they met their first boat and had to pull in to a passing-place to let it go by—a black, battered craft, drawn by a tired-looking horse that munched from a pail as it walked, and steered by an old, old man as motionless at the tiller as though he'd been hewn out of granite. Then came a stretch of half a mile or more that was covered with duckweed, a brilliant green carpet through which they cut a black swath; and twice Hugh had to clean out the water filter. From there on, it was easy going to Autherley Junction, which they reached about four. They were now on the very threshold of Wolverhampton, but separated from it by a flight of twenty-one locks in a row, which Hugh felt very thankful he hadn't to tackle. Their own route turned off sharply to the right, under a bridge. Immediately beyond, a toll lock with a rise of only a few inches took them through on to the Shropshire Union, and a friendly toll clerk stamped their permit and welcomed them like a host.

The new canal was much straighter than anything they had been on yet, and looked like a water artery of importance. It had been built, so the guide-book said, by the famous Telford, whose method was to cross valleys on embankments and drive cuttings through ridges—in contrast to his equally famous predecessor Brindley, who had built the Stour Cut and would go miles round to avoid an obstacle. The Shropshire Union was also much wider, though—as Mr. Flint had warned—the margins proved shallow and the width deceptive. But the visual effect was pleasing. They were high up, now—three hundred feet or more above sea level—and from the cabin top of *Varley* they had a panoramic view over farms and fields and villages, right across to the dominating peak of the Wrekin. For the moment, the intimacy, the sense of isolation, the elusive charm had gone; this canal had a business-like air. Its banks had been strengthened with concrete piling and corrugated metal sheets, and at one point they came across a dredger at work. The traffic was patchy, but they met two strings of working boats and a pleasure boat in the course of the first hour. Clare was alert and watchful, and scrutinized each one closely as it glided by. She, too, had a businesslike air.

They moored that night near a village called Wheaton Aston, seven miles along the canal. There was a lock there, a splendidly kept lock, the first step down from the summit level, and after a brief discussion they decided to make it their temporary headquarters. It seemed an ideal place to start their inquiries.

From now on they concentrated their whole attention on the working boats and their occupants. There was rather less traffic than Mr. Sears had led them to expect, with long gaps between arrivals, but when the lock was active, it was very active indeed. Sometimes the boats would come in a string, the combined tack-tack of their diesel engines announcing their approach from far away. More often they came in pairs, the second one an engineless "butty" towed by the first. Most of them had become the property of British Waterways as a result of nationalisation and were painted a uniform blue and yellow. All seemed to be of a standard size—seven feet wide, and seventy feet long, to fit the locks, with the front fifty feet or so serving as cargo space. All were built to the same pattern, with bluff bows, and tall rudder posts called "ram's heads," and shapely, curving tiller bars and elaborately lettered names. All had the same low, cramped-looking cabin in the stern, with a coal fire inside and a chimney sticking up from the roof. It seemed to Clare that a single cabin, however ingeniously the space was used, would hardly be sufficient to accommodate "A" and his wife and Lucy, as well as the baby—but a boat and butty would have been just right, and that often seemed to be the family unit.

One thing that comforted her a little was the discovery that her harrowing mental picture of unrelieved dirt and squalor on the cut was far from an accurate one. When families were dirty, they were *very* dirty—but that was exceptional. Most of the canal folk—and particularly, Clare soon learned, those who had been born to the life—took the greatest pride in keeping their boats scrupulously clean and attractive. The traditional roses and castles had largely disappeared, but the gipsy love of colour and brightness still showed itself in the gorgeously decorated water cans and the wealth of polished metal. Many of the cabin tops carried painted flower boxes and jam jars filled with bunches of wild flowers from the banks. Often there was a canary in a swinging cage to add to the gaiety. The cabins themselves, though tiny, looked very cosy, with their glowing stoves and gleaming pans and shining brass. Occasionally, glancing down through the double doors without appearing to pry, Clare would get a revealing glimpse of polished table flaps and crumb trays, of spotless lace and pretty hanging plates.

The canal folk varied more than the boats. There were morose old men with cutty pipes, rough and earthy in their cloth caps and nondescript working clothes, who looked at *Varley* and spat powerfully into the cut. There were younger and more cheerful ones, stripped to the waist, with tanned backs and bare heads and a ready grin for Clare. There were proud and handsome ones, with lean brown features and dark Romany eyes and earrings. There were middle-aged mothers, plump and serene and immensely competent at the tiller, and adolescent girls strangely garbed in nylons and gum-boots and hair-curlers, and a few slatterns who nagged and scolded. There were happy, healthy youngsters who raced along the towpath with windlasses to prepare the lock, and quite a number of small babies. Very occasionally, Clare would draw Hugh's attention to some really tough types, people who looked as though they might be capable of anything, people who seemed more like the popular conception of a "bargee." But for the most part the folk who came through in the boats appeared as law-abiding and respectable as Mr. Chappell's neighbours in Mill Hill.

As far as establishing contact with them was concerned, it soon became apparent that Mr. Sears's advice had been sound. The boatmen, with their shared hardships, their strong sense of community, and their independence, formed a pretty exclusive club, and would never be easy for a stranger to get to know quickly, but Clare and Hugh were as well placed as any stranger could be. Here, with their own narrow boat moored near the lock, and at least a smattering of knowledge about the cut and its ways, they were usually considered worthy of a few minutes' chat. The lock itself was a perfect place for their task. Though the boatmen showed an enviable skill and speed in getting through it, even they had to wait while it filled and emptied. Sometimes

Hugh would tentatively give help at the gates; sometimes he would produce a cigarette as a boatman waited with his broad bottom against the balance beam. Sometimes a group of shy but interested children would stand to be photographed, while Clare talked to the mothers. There were hazards about every new approach, and not all were successful, but a little tact generally smoothed the way. A proper humility about pleasure boats, they discovered, helped enormously; the gambit of "I expect you find us a frightful nuisance" was particularly effective. And few of the boatmen minded having their expertise admired, their advice sought, especially if it was Clare who sought it. Little by little, the scraps of information that emerged built up into quite a picture of life on the cut, and the knowledge was useful for later exchanges. The men talked, in broad dialects that were sometimes hard to follow, of the wretched state many of the canals had been allowed to get into, and of the difficulties they encountered on the routes. Some who'd been brought up in the job told how they'd tried factory work instead, and how the rush and noise had made them nervous and sent them back to the boats with relief. And the women talked of young wives from "off the land" who often didn't take to the life because of the cramped conditions and constant exposure, and of new-fangled ideas that some people had about schooling for the children, and of winter hardships.

Whenever it seemed that a friendly basis was established, Clare and Hugh put their crucial questions with directness. Usually their story was received with interest and a warm sympathy. It was the answers that were depressing, the emphatic headshakes. None of the boatmen or their wives had seen or heard anything of a family with an unexplained baby on board, though many of them had been travelling up or down this particular cut at the very time when "A" would have been using it. None of them had come across such a family as Clare described—a man and two women, one of them named Lucy, newcomers to the cut. If they had, they said, they would have been pretty sure to notice, because they reckoned to know everybody on the boats—and, anyway, there weren't many new people. The drift was mostly the other way. Still, they'd keep a lookout, they'd pass the word about it up and down. News travelled fast on the cut. . . .

For three days, hardly a boat went through unquestioned, except for the odd one or two that slipped by after dark. When there was shopping to be done, or a letter posted, or a phone call made to Mr. Flint to see if there were any messages, either Hugh or Clare always stayed behind at the lock and got on with the job. But by now the eager hopes that had sustained Clare on the trip from Blampton were beginning to fade. It wasn't just the succession of "No's" that dispirited her so much—if it had merely been a question of holding on for the lucky "Yes" she would have been prepared to continue indefinitely. What dismayed her was every family's certainty that they *would* have known—the corollary being that there was nothing to know. The conviction was growing in her that she and Hugh were on the wrong track. The logic that had brought them to the working boats had seemed sound enough at Llangollen—but somewhere along the line there must be a fault. For now that she was so much more familiar with the life of the cut, it seemed most unlikely to her that Arnold—who must also have known a good deal about it—would have tried to hide Christine among a body of people who knew each other, and each other's affairs, so intimately.

Round about one in the morning, on the fourth night at Wheaton Aston, Hugh suddenly found himself wide awake. He had been disturbed, he thought, by some unusual sound in the boat. He lay listening; and presently he heard it again. It was Clare, and she was crying.

After a moment he put on his dressing-gown and went in to her. Moonlight was streaming through the cabin window, touching her pillow, and her face looked white and woebegone.

He dropped down on the edge of the bunk and took her hand. "Don't cry, Clare," he said. "Please don't cry."

"Oh, Hugh," she sobbed, "I'm so afraid. I don't believe we'll ever find her . . . If you know how I felt—it's like an awful ache, all the time."

"We'll find her," he said gently. "You've got to believe that."

"I *do* try—but it all seems so hopeless."

He put an arm round her shoulders and drew her close to him. "You'll feel better in the morning."

"But we don't seem to be getting anywhere at all. . . ." The tears still flowed. Hugh sat holding her tightly, trying to think of something to say that would comfort her. But it wasn't easy.

"We've got to be patient, Clare. I know it's hard—I know just how you're feeling. But it's the only way—just to keep plodding on. If one thing doesn't work we'll have to try and think of something else."

She began to dry her eyes. "Oh, Hugh, you've been an angel—I don't know what I'd have done without you. I'm sorry to seem so ungrateful."

"Don't be silly, darling. You've got to have someone's shoulder to cry on now and again—and why not mine? You know I love you, don't you?"

She stared at him. "Why, Hugh . . ."

"Didn't you know . . .? I always have. Right from the first moment we met."

"I didn't know. . . ." She continued to stare. "Why didn't you ever say?"

"I guess I arrived on the scene too late. You were completely mesmerised by that high-pressure salesman of yours—there didn't seem a chance for an inarticulate type like me. . . . Anyway, there it is—you know now."

"But—we've always been such friends."

"The two things don't necessarily rule each other out."

"But I never thought of you in that way at all . . . Never!"

"You needn't be so emphatic," he said ruefully. "It's perfectly obvious. If you *had*, you wouldn't have come away with me alone on a boat without giving it a second thought. And you certainly wouldn't be sitting there now in a transparent nightie as unconcerned as though I were the district nurse!"

"Hugh!" Clare slid down under the bedclothes. "I don't call *that* being inarticulate!" She looked at him as though she were seeing him for the first time.

"And I always thought of you as so reliable!" she murmured.

He grinned. "Don't worry, I'm not planning to make a pass at you. Not at the moment, anyway. Forget it."

"I don't know that I want to. . . ." she said slowly. "Heavens, Hugh, how stupid I must have seemed to you all this time!"

"Oh, no. Just preoccupied."

"But I should have noticed."

"There's been nothing to notice. . . . Look, Clare, I didn't intend to spring this on you—I hope you're not going to let it worry you."

"Why should it worry me?"

"You don't want to call it a day?—with, the boat, I mean?"

"Not because of this, Hugh. Not if you think we can still do any good with it. . . . *Do* you?"

He hesitated. "Well—the cut was always a pretty slim hope, you know."

"You thought it was worth trying, though."

"I couldn't think of anything better. For that matter, I still can't. . . . And I thought it would help you not to fret."

"I know," she said. "You've been terribly kind."

"Don't fool yourself," Hugh said, and got up. "I'm not all that kind. Right now you'd be horrified at what I'm feeling . . . I think it's time I took myself off."

"Oh, Hugh . . ." Clare gave a little smile. "Anyway, you were quite right—it *has* helped to take my mind off things. In any other circumstances it could have been fun—I like being on a boat with you. If only Christine had been here. . . ."

"We'll try it again some time, when she is."

"Wouldn't that be wonderful?"

He drew the curtain across the window, cutting off the moonlight. "Good night, Clare," he said. "Sleep well."

"Good night, Hugh."

He was just getting into his bunk when she called out, "Hugh!"

"Yes?" he said.

"I like being with you anyway, boat or no boat!"

Neither of them made any direct reference next day to what had happened during the night, and there was no striking change in the atmosphere aboard *Varley*. The easy comradeship, which had been a habit with them for so long, was only slightly disturbed. Hugh was a shade more tender and solicitous. Clare, inevitably, had a greater awareness of him. But her constant and over-riding thought was still of Christine, and for the moment the search was all that mattered.

At breakfast they reviewed the whole position. Clare told Hugh why she'd begun to lose hope of the working boats. Hugh was inclined to agree with her—he'd been thinking along the same lines himself—but he suggested they should move on and try their luck in one more place before giving up the cut altogether. There was a junction at Barbridge, he pointed out, farther along the Shropshire Union, where they might be able to make contact with boats travelling between the Potteries and the ports, in addition to those going direct from Wolverhampton. Clare nodded, having no better plan to propose. At least they would be breaking fresh ground.

They set off early, for though the morning was brilliant, the forecast spoke of rain. There were no more locks, and for mile after mile the cut ran straight as a military road. It was surprisingly empty, too—for the first time since they'd reached the Shropshire Union they saw no traffic whatever. After a while Hugh left Clare to do the steering and took his sketchbook on to the foredeck. It was the pleasantest place on the boat when they were under way, for the engine was inaudible and there was almost no sense of motion, just a faint ripple under the bows, and the eye could concentrate undisturbed on the scene immediately ahead. A peaceful hour passed. Then they left the high embankment on which they'd been travelling and plunged into a deep cutting, with tall magnificent bridges and steep banks clothed with dense, untrodden woods, a sanctuary for birds. Once Hugh jumped up excitedly, pointing into the trees, and Clare saw for the first time the vivid blue flash of a kingfisher.

Their smooth passage was checked after a while by the first craft of the day—a working boat that seemed to have come to a stop under a bridge. Clare slipped the gear lever into neutral and let

Varley glide slowly up to it. As the gap narrowed she saw that there were in fact two boats, heading in the same direction as *Varley*. Presumably they had passed Wheaton Aston during the hours of darkness, for their appearance was unfamiliar. The second, a butty, was one of the most colourful that Clare had seen. The long tiller bar was striped red, white and blue like a barber's pole; the stove funnel was brass-ringed with a brass safety chain; the tall drinking-water can on the after deck was beautifully decorated and varnished. A great bunch of dog-daisies stood in a jar on the cabin top.

Clare steered in gently beside the butty's cabin until *Varley's* bows touched the ground, and then went forward to join Hugh and see what was happening. As the boat swung lightly against the butty's stern, a handsome, middle-aged woman suddenly stuck her head out of the cabin hatch. She had a lilac scarf over her hair, and wore a bright checked cotton frock and a green cardigan. The sleeves were rolled above her elbows, revealing powerful forearms. She inspected *Varley* and its occupants closely for a moment or two, and then gave a cautious nod of greeting. A girl popped up beside her, the two of them quite filling the hatch. The girl was in her early twenties, and had a sulky-attractive face and thick waving hair.

"How d'ye do?" Hugh said, and smiled at the girl. Her face lost its sulky look and she smiled back, shyly.

"What's happened?" Hugh asked.

"We're stemmed up," said the woman, jerking her head towards the boat in front.

"Stemmed up. . . .?"

"Aye, we're aground." She sounded quite philosophical about it,

"I see. . . ." Hugh suddenly realised why they'd met no traffic during the morning. "Have you been here long?"

"All night!" The woman sniffed. "They overloaded us. We told 'em they were putting too much in, but they would keep on. . . . Think they know everything, those chaps. . . ." She had a strong accent—Liverpool, Hugh thought—but her voice was pleasant.

"What'll happen now?" Clare asked.

"I dunno. P'raps they'll fetch a tug. They got us into it, so they'll have to get us out of it."

A few spots of rain had begun to fall and a wind was stirring the tops of the trees. A light puff caught *Varley*'s bows, swinging her free of the ground, and Hugh took the shaft to hold the boat in position. The woman said, "You'll be better tied up to us," and with a deft movement she made the butty's stern strap fast to *Varley*. "We'll be here for a good while, like as not."

Hugh nodded. The bridge was completely blocked—there was nothing they could do, even if they'd wanted to. "Well, we're not in a great hurry," he said. "I dare say you are, though."

The woman shrugged, then smiled at her daughter. "Phoebe wants to get to Manchester, don't you, Phoebe?" Her tone was teasing.

Phoebe looked haughty.

Hugh said, "Boy friend waiting?" with a grin that disarmed.

"Aye, there's a young chap hanging his hat for her. . . . A mechanic! I reckon she's not long for the cut!"

"Oh, Mum!" said Phoebe.

They had got on good terms so quickly that Clare felt she could safely raise the subject of Christine, but at that moment the rain became a deluge and she and Hugh were forced to leave the open foredeck and take shelter. Through the double doors, they watched developments under the bridge. Three men were talking together on the towpath, and a second boat seemed to be manoeuvring just beyond the arch, with others stationary behind it. Mum had gone below, but presently she popped up again with an umbrella and stood in the rain with her head out of the hatch, quite happy and unconcerned. After a while a little man with a bright, pink face came walking down the towpath and exchanged some words with her in an accent even broader than her own. Neither Hugh nor Clare was able to follow the conversation, but Hugh caught the word "unload." Phoebe emerged in gum-boots and a mackintosh and helped Mum to fix a long gangplank from the butty to the shore, and the man came splashing aboard, careless of wet feet. A fragrant smell of stew was beginning to come from the butty's cabin, and Hugh and Clare decided they might as well have some food themselves.

By the time they'd finished lunch, there were new signs of activity outside. An empty lighter was creeping up astern of them, bow-hauled by two men. The pink-faced husband went ashore and the gang-plank was drawn in and the lighter slid slowly past *Varley* and along to the bridge. More working boats were now visible through the arch, and there appeared to be some congestion. Several men began to unload boxes from the grounded boat and transfer them to the lighter.

Around one o'clock, the rain suddenly stopped, and Hugh and Clare went out on to the foredeck again. Almost at once, the two women popped up. Hugh offered them cigarettes, and the girl accepted. He gave her a light, and then plunged into the familiar routine.

"I expect you know most of the people on the boats, don't you?" he said.

"We know 'em all," Mum said; and added grimly, "Some good, some bad."

"I suppose there are bad ones?"

"There's always bad 'uns—everywhere. You soon get to sort 'em out, though."

Hugh nodded. "I wonder if you've seen some people we're looking for? Three people—a man and two women, with a baby a year old. . . ."

"On a boat, you mean?"

"Yes. They'd be strangers to you, probably—we think they might have just come on the cut for the first time."

Mum looked thoughtful. "Up this way?"

"Yes—we think they might have been around here about three weeks ago."

"What are they like?"

"Well, that's just the trouble—we don't know. . . ." Briefly, Hugh explained the circumstances of Christine's disappearance. Both women gazed at Clare, their faces full of interest and kindly concern. But they couldn't help.

"We haven't seen anyone new off the land, have we, Phoebe . . . ? Not these last few weeks?"

Phoebe shook her head.

"If there had been anyone," Hugh said, "a family like that, would you have noticed, do you think?"

"Aye, we'd have noticed all right, if they'd come by. We know all the folk—all the boats."

Hugh nodded. It was the old story.

"One of the women would be called Lucy," he said. "I suppose you don't happen to know of a Lucy on the cut, do you?"

Mum frowned, looking at Phoebe. "Do we know a Lucy . . . ? I reckon there must be lots o' Lucys—but it's the faces you remember more than the names. . . ."

Phoebe said: "I know a boat called *Lucy*."

"A boat. . . . ?"

"Yes, a pleasure boat—one of them cruisers. Remember, Mum, that old thing at Gailey?"

"That's right," Mum said. "Back in the spring, it was, by Gailey Lock. We was taking some stuff up through the Stour Cut when this one was stopped. . . ."

She broke off as a sudden hail came from one of the men ahead and the diesel in the front boat started up.

"Well, here we go," she said. She cast off *Varley* and gripped the big striped tiller. "Cheerio!—and good luck to you. We'll keep an eye open." Phoebe smiled, and gave a little wave, and the butty moved slowly off through the bridge.

Chapter Five

Once more, Clare was scrutinising the well-worn message. They had passed through the arch and tied up fifty yards beyond it, out of the way of the traffic.

"I don't see why Lucy *shouldn't* be a boat," she said, after a moment. "It makes sense all right that way. . . . In fact, I'm not sure it doesn't make more sense."

"Why do you say that?"

"Well, take this bit about 'giving trouble.' A boat could easily 'give trouble,' couldn't it, but if a woman were complaining about things and demanding more money, wouldn't it be more usual to say she was 'making trouble'?"

Hugh savoured the two phrases. "M'm!—I don't know. Perhaps."

"Anyway," Clare said, "two people would have been far more satisfactory from Arnold's point of view. Having a third person around would have added to the risk almost as much as giving Christine to two separate families—I'm sure he'd have wanted to avoid that. A man and wife would have been the obvious arrangement."

"That's certainly true."

"Then let's see how it goes. . . .'A' could be someone who knew about canals but didn't live on them—some one who worked at Arnold's wharf, perhaps. He'd still talk about the 'cut,' so that would be all right. Arnold persuades him to go and live on a boat called *Lucy*, with his wife and Christine. 'A' doesn't mind the life, but the boat gives trouble and the wife decides she won't put up with the discomfort unless they're paid more. . . . That's all right, isn't it?"

"It makes sense of the message, I agree," Hugh said, "but it's the purest speculation. The only thing we know for certain is that there's a boat called *Lucy*!"

"We know more than that, Hugh. We know that a particular boat called *Lucy* was at Gailey in the spring, and she may still have been there in June, and Gailey's not far from Wolverhampton where the message was posted. And we know she's not there any longer, or we'd have seen her ourselves when we passed through."

"She'd probably be on the move at this time of year in any case," Hugh said. "The owner may be taking his holiday on her. Or he may let her all through the summer, the way Flint lets this one."

"Then why shouldn't he have let her to Arnold?"

"Arnold wouldn't have known he wanted a boat until June—and we know how difficult it is to hire a boat suddenly in the middle of the season."

"We managed to."

"That was just luck."

"Arnold could have been lucky, too."

"He *could*," Hugh said.

"The thing is, Hugh, we didn't arrive at our canal theory without a lot of good reasons, and most of them still stand if we substitute a pleasure boat for a working boat—and everything else fits much better. A pleasure boat would have been far safer from Arnold's point of view than a working boat because there'd have been no reason for the canal folk to pay any particular attention to it. . . . It seems extraordinary we never thought of it before."

Hugh grunted. "Somehow one doesn't associate pleasure cruising with the sort of people who sent that message."

"I suppose that's it, but then it wouldn't have been their idea, of course—Arnold would have been the one to suggest it and make all the arrangements.   Anyway, Hugh, I'm sure it's worth looking into. Couldn't we go over to Gailey and make some inquiries? We might be able to talk to the owner."

"We'll probably find he's let the boat to a judge or a parson."

"Then that'll be that, but at least we'll know."

"Okay," Hugh said. "I've no objection."

"After all, we have given the working boat idea a pretty thorough test, and I don't really think we're likely to do any better at Barbridge. ... What's the quickest way to get to Gailey?"

Hugh spread out the map and studied it for a moment. "Well, there's a village only about a mile from here. We could walk in and see if we could get a bus."

"Right!" Clare said. "Let's go."

There was no convenient bus to Gailey, but the postmistress in the village post office had the number of a local man who ran a taxi service and she rang him up while they waited. In ten minutes his car was at the door, and twenty minutes later he was setting them down by Gailey lock.

There were plenty of people to ask about *Lucy*. Adjoining the lock there was a pleasant little tea house, and on the main road above the lock there was a shop, and on the opposite bank there were several cottages. They tried them all, but they got most of their information from an affable housewife at one of the cottages. She remembered *Lucy* very well—an old, neglected motor cruiser, she said, that had been moored for a long time about two hundred yards above the lock on the side away from the towpath. Far from having been let out on hire, it had remained there derelict and apparently forgotten for over a year. It was owned, she thought, by someone in London, and there had been a rumour that he'd wanted to sell it. She didn't know who the owner was. She did know that nobody had been near the boat for a long while, until suddenly, a month or two back, it had disappeared. One day it had been there, and the next it hadn't, and nobody around had any idea what had happened to it. When Hugh pressed her to try and remember just when it had disappeared, she thought for a bit, and went and consulted her daughter, and finally decided that it must have been some time in early June.

Clare was elated. "You see," she said, as they turned back towards the waiting taxi, "it needn't have been just luck if Arnold was able to get hold of her. She could have been advertised for sale, and he could have bought her—or 'A' could, for him, if he didn't want to use his own name. Then 'A' could have come up and taken her away secretly, so that he wouldn't have to answer questions and leave a trail behind him. . . . You must admit it's very suspicious the way she was spirited off—and at the right time, too, early June!"

"It's certainly surprising," Hugh agreed. "With all these people around, it seems extraordinary she was able to get away without anyone knowing."

"She was probably moved at night."

"I should think she must have been," Hugh said thoughtfully. "She could have been poled along for a bit of course, and there aren't any more locks until Autherley, so once she was away she'd have had a clear run."

"Hugh, I'm sure it's worth while trying to find out something more about her. . . . Perhaps the canal authorities could help us?"

Hugh considered. "They'd probably be able to give us the name and address of the owner—and of the new owner, too, if she's changed hands—but I don't know that it would get us very far."

"We could go and see him."

"If he's not 'A,' there'd be no point. If he is 'A,' he's presumbly aboard *Lucy*. If we're going to make inquiries at all, the obvious thing is to try and find the boat."

"Yes, I see . . . All right, then, where do we start to look?"

"Well," Hugh said, after a moment, "I suppose the best place to begin would be the Welsh canal, because if there's anything in this new idea, that's where *Lucy* went to. . . . As a matter of fact, it is just the sort of place they would have made for if their plan was to lie up quietly all the summer. No working boats, hardly any traffic, nice quiet moorings—and a holiday background to give them cover."

Clare nodded. "Hugh—isn't this where that eighteen mile business comes in again?"

"It could be—though I don't suppose she'd have stayed on in the same spot all this time."

"Probably not, but if that was the rendezvous three weeks ago and she was there for two days, someone might remember her and be able to tell us who was aboard and then we'd know whether there was any point in going on looking."

"True. . . ."

"At least it's as good a jumping-off place as any."

Hugh gazed at her eager face. "Clare darling, don't build too much on this, will you?—the whole thing seems frightfully shaky to me. After all, anyone could have bought *Lucy* and taken her away at night—some enthusiastic young fellow anxious to get started on his holiday. . . ."

"We'll find her and see," Clare said.

Hugh nodded slowly. "Well, if we're going to be doing a lot of chasing about," he said, "I think we ought to get the cars. We can easily find some place to park them near *Varley*, and we'll be mobile then. . . ."

"Good idea, Hugh. Let's go and get them now."

They paid off the taxi at Mr. Flint's wharf and walked quickly across to his office. When he saw who it was he looked even more worried than on the last occasion, but they soon satisfied him that they were in no trouble with *Varley* and that they merely wanted to take a trip or two round the countryside for a change. They collected the cars and headed straight back for the boat, which they reached in less than twenty minutes.

As soon as they were aboard, Hugh got out the maps they had used when they'd been checking up on the marked points round Llangollen, and spread out the one that covered the canal area. He studied it for a few moments, going over one or two of the measurements again. Then he said: "Well, according to the crosses we made before, there's no point on any direct route from Llangollen that touches the canal *exactly* eighteen miles away. There's a stretch south of a village called Welshampton that I make about nineteen. Otherwise, there's nothing."

"I should think that's near enough," Clare said. "We agreed before that Arnold might not have wanted to take his car right to the canal. Let's go and see, anyway."

It took them three quarters of an hour to reach Welshampton. Hugh remembered the place, which had been one of the points in his sector during the earlier search—a mere hamlet, with a shop or two and a pub where he had made his inquiries about new arrivals in the district. They stopped again, this time to ask about *Lucy*, but the name meant nothing to anyone. Clare's hope that someone from the boat might have shopped in the village proved an empty one—it seemed there'd been no one off the cut for quite a while. Presently they drove on, reaching the canal at a place where it ran beside a lake called Cole Mere. It was an attractive spot in the late afternoon, with bright sun sparkling on the water and dappling the towpath through a narrow belt of conifers and oak. To save time, they decided to walk in opposite directions along the cut and to turn after half an hour and join up again at the starting point.

When they met an hour later, neither of them had anything to report. There had been no sign of a boat—no sign, indeed, of life at all, except for the birds on the mere. Not a soul had appeared in sight. It was one of the loveliest, but also one of the quietest reaches they had come across.

"Well, we knew we probably wouldn't find her here after all this time," Clare said, determined not to seem disappointed. "We'll just have to go on looking, that's all."

Hugh gazed up and down the silent cut. "The thing is, where?"

"Let's try and put ourselves in 'A's' position," Clare suggested after a moment. "Look, suppose *you'd* been 'A' and you'd brought *Lucy* up here to lie low, and then you'd had this meeting with Arnold and fixed everything up for quite a time ahead—what would *you* have done afterwards?"

Hugh considered. "I'm not sure I wouldn't have cleared off back down the cut," he said. "After a meeting like that I should think there'd have been a strong urge to put a little distance between one's self and any possible inquiries."

"Don't forget 'A' had no idea that Arnold was going to be arrested," Clare said. "He probably didn't expect any inquiries. In any case, the chance that someone would think of a boat must have seemed pretty small. Wouldn't he have felt reasonably safe?"

"I still think that if it had been me I'd have got out of the immediate neighbourhood," Hugh said. "I don't mean I'd have rushed off in a panic, but I'd have kept on the move. . . . Mind you, there is the other side of the picture—if I'd specifically chosen the Welsh canal because it seemed an ideal retreat, I suppose I'd have been reluctant to leave. . . . I might even have argued that a bold advance towards Llangollen would have been the surest way of avoiding suspicion!"

"Heavens!—that leaves it all pretty open, doesn't it?"

"Really, yes."

"Well," Clare said thoughtfully, "we're certainly not going to feel very happy searching *down* the cut if there's the slightest possibility that *Lucy* may be behind us."

There was a little pause. Then Hugh said: "You know, Clare, if we're going to take this search seriously I think the thing to do is to start at Llangollen. According to the map, the canal ends just above the town, so if we worked down from there at least we'd know that *Lucy* was in front of us—always assuming, of course, that the whole thing isn't a wild goose chase."

"What would we do?" Clare asked. "Walk along the towpath?"

"Well, now, let's see . . ." Hugh consulted the map again. "We *could* use the cars, I suppose. There are several places where the canal runs parallel to roads—we might be able to cover those without even getting out."

"What about the other bits?"

"We could drive from bridge to bridge—that way we'd probably get a clear view of quite long stretches without actually having to walk them. . . . Still, doing the whole thing on foot would give us far more opportunities of talking to people, and it wouldn't take all that long with two of us at it. We could organise a sort of relay system."

"How do you mean?"

"Well, one of us would start walking from Llangollen, say, to a bridge five miles along the cut. The other would take a car, drive to the bridge and park there, and walk on to another bridge about five miles ahead. The first person would pick up the car at the end of the five miles, drive to the second bridge, and collect the other person. That would halve the walking distance for both of us and save bags of time."

Clare nodded. "It sounds much the best way to me."

"All right," Hugh said. "Then let's get along to Llangollen and make a start."

They began their inquiries at the spot where the canal idea had first occurred to them—the Waterside Café. Once Mr. Sears had heard their story he quite saw the advantages of a pleasure boat over a working boat as a place to hide a child, but he said he hadn't seen or heard anything of a boat named *Lucy* and she certainly hadn't been up as far as Llangollen. He promised to get in touch with one or two friends on the cut and see if he could find out something about her, and they thanked him warmly. Then they set off on the first stage of their search. By now there was scarcely enough daylight left to make the relay system worth starting, and they decided to cover the first few miles of the cut together by car. One of the main roads out of Llangollen ran close to the canal for nearly two miles, and when it finally turned away a secondary road served them almost as well. From time to time they had to stop and make their way on foot to the towpath to get a clear view, but they still managed to cover the ground quite fast. They passed a few of Mr. Sears's rowing-boats, and a number of late strollers on the bank, but that was all. Then it grew dark, and they had to suspend the search and return to *Varley*.

They were back on the job soon after daylight next morning, starting again at the point where they had left off. This time they had brought only one of the cars with them, and they put the relay system into operation right away. Hugh gave himself the first five-mile leg, which promised to be a little arduous, and Clare went off with the car and the map to park at the appointed bridge and continue with the next leg. Some ninety minutes later they met according to plan and briefly exchanged experiences before continuing on their way. Hugh's section had been spectacular—at a place called Pontcysyllte the canal had been carried across the broad valley of the river Dee by a narrow iron aqueduct perched dizzily on high stone pillars, with mountains all around and turbulent water roaring below. A little farther on, it had plunged into a steep hillside, and for a quarter of a mile Hugh had had to grope his way through an unlit tunnel, with water pouring on him from the roof and only a handrail beside the towpath to guide him. By contrast, Clare's first section had passed through empty, tranquil country, and her walk had been almost without incident. She had talked to two girls on a field-track bridge, two small boys fishing with jam jars and nets, and one labourer cutting a drain. There had been no news of *Lucy*.

The next stage took much longer. Early on, Clare came across a canal-side village and spent some time there making inquiries. She also stopped at a lock cottage, and again to talk to two men unloading puddle clay from a British Waterways service boat—though in each case without useful result. Hugh, who had taken the lead on this leg, had a few words with an elderly couple whom he hailed from the bank as they cruised slowly up the cut in a pleasure boat called *Eider Duck*. They had left the Shropshire Union a fortnight ago, they said, and had seen quite a lot of cruisers on their way up—perhaps eight or ten, altogether—but they could remember none called *Lucy*. It was a depressing encounter, for at best it seemed to mean that *Lucy* had got well clear of the Welsh canal, and at worst that she'd never been on it at all—which Hugh thought the more likely. Almost certainly, he decided, this *was* a wild goose chase. He continued on his way in a melancholy frame of mind, passing again the stretch by Cole Mere that he and Clare had covered on the previous day, and reaching the five-mile bridge well ahead of the car.

It was nearly noon when Clare turned up. She asked about the cruiser, which had passed her near the end of her section, and she listened in silence to Hugh's account of his talk with the couple. She was obviously tired from the unaccustomed exercise and the blank miles, and presently Hugh suggested lunch. They found a grassy bank near the bridge, and ate their sandwiches, and over a cigarette they planned the next leg of the search. They rested for half an hour, and then prepared to set off again. This time Clare was to walk on, and Hugh was to take the car. He strolled through the bridge with her, wishing they didn't have to keep on separating. Just beyond the arch they came suddenly upon the first angler of the day—a boy of twelve or thirteen, scarcely visible among bushes, sitting engrossed beside his creel. They stopped, and Hugh put the usual question—"I suppose you haven't seen anything of a boat called *Lucy?*"

For a moment the boy didn't answer, and they thought he hadn't understood. He was silently regarding his float. Then he said, in an attractively sing-song voice,

"Yes, I have."

"You *have!*" Hugh gazed at him in utter astonishment. "When?"

The boy thought, but not for long. "It was three weeks ago," he said. "On a Monday. I remember, see, because I was fishing. I can always remember the days when I am fishing."

"Are you sure *Lucy* was the name?"

"Yes, I am quite sure. A dirty old cruiser, she was."

"Where did you see her?"

The boy jerked his head. "Down the cut," he said. "Moored against the towpath, she was, about a mile down. I passed her when I came here to fish. It was in the morning."

Clare dropped down beside him on the grass, her heart pounding. "Did you notice if there was a baby on board?"

"A baby? No, I don't think there was any baby. There was just a chap on his own."

"Oh!"

Hugh said: "Did you pass her again when you went home?"

"Yes, at dinner time."

"And was the chap still on his own then?"

"Yes, he was."

"Did you see the boat again?"

"No, I didn't. When I came by next time, she had gone away." The boy drew in his line, and inspected the bait, and made another cast.

After a moment, Hugh said, "What was this chap like?—can you tell me?"

The boy wrinkled his brown forehead. "Well, he was so dirty, see, it is hard to say. Grease and oil all over him, he had, and his head bent down over the engine and a spanner in his hand. There was something wrong with it, I am sure."

"Good lord!" said Hugh softly. He felt the sudden, eager pressure of Clare's hand on his arm. "Did the man speak to you?"

"No, he didn't say a word, he was too busy, see. Very surly, he looked."

"Do you remember which way the boat was pointing?"

"She was pointing up the cut, where you have come from."

"I see . . ." Hugh's face was expressionless. "Well, thank you very much indeed—we're most grateful to you. And we hope you catch a lot of fish!"

"So we *were* right!" Clare said. All the fatigue had left her face; her voice was eager. "Oh, Hugh, I'm sure we're getting somewhere at last."

Hugh was cautious. He looked as though he still hadn't quite got over his surprise. "What about the chap being on his own?" he said.

"I don't think that's much to go by, really. After all, if he knew he was going to be tinkering with the engine all morning, he'd have wanted to be left on his own, wouldn't he? He could easily have sent his wife off somewhere with Christine."

"He could, I suppose."

"Hugh, it was the right day, do you realise that? It was the second day of Arnold's stay at Llangollen. The right day, the right canal—*and* a boat that was giving trouble. You're not going to say that was all coincidence?"

"I don't know—this canal *is* a favourite cruising ground, after all, and *Lucy* had to be somewhere on that day, and I imagine lots of old boats give trouble. . . ." Hugh stood frowning. "All the same, it's certainly interesting about the dicky engine. That could be the answer to all sorts of things that haven't made much sense before."

"How do you mean?"

"It could be the explanation of all that dashing around that Arnold did. Remember we never quite understood what business could have kept him hanging about here for two days when he was so desperately anxious to get abroad?"

Clare nodded.

"Well, if the boat he intended to meet had had a last-minute breakdown on the way to the rendezvous, he might have been *looking* for it—more or less the way we've been doing. On the first day he could have failed to find it, and on the second day he could have succeeded."

"Hugh—that *is* an idea."

"It does seem more plausible than two meetings at the same spot, doesn't it? And he might well have knocked up seventy miles in two days, because on his own he'd probably have used the technique we began with when we left Llangollen—staying with the car as much as possible and walking to the bridges when he had to.... Incidentally, if he expected to be searching along a lonely canal each day and knew he hadn't a moment to lose, that might explain the packed lunches, too."

"But of course. ..."

"And that's not all, either." Hugh was being carried along now on a wave of ideas. "The boat was still heading for Llangollen. Perhaps the original rendezvous *was* Llangollen. If so, that would take care of another loose end—the casual way Arnold seemed to rely on picking up a self-drive car in the middle of the holiday season."

"You mean he wouldn't have expected to need one?"

"Exactly. He could have planned to stop off at Llangollen for one night, meet 'A' at the boat after dark according to a prearranged schedule, have a quick talk, and go straight off to Ireland next day."

"But Hugh, that's fine—now it *does* all fit. ...Why do you look so doubtful?"

The wave had spent itself. Hugh said, "I suppose because it seems too good to be true."

"That's pure superstition."

"Not entirely. Things do begin to fit, I agree—but then a lot of things seemed to fit the working boat idea, until we started to investigate. The same thing could happen again."

"I don't think it will," Clare said. "Anyway, we'll find *Lucy*, and then we'll know."

All through the afternoon they continued their search down the cut. They were in much better heart, now, for though they had no idea where *Lucy* was they felt they were following a warm trail at last and could reasonably expect to come upon fresh traces of her at any moment, if not upon the boat itself. If they could get hold of just one solid piece of evidence, Hugh said, like meeting someone who remembered seeing a baby on board, he would be in favour of going back to the police and trying to get them to join in the search. Until then, the best thing seemed to be to push ahead on their own—and they did so unsparingly. Clare was driven on now by a new sense of urgency, as well as by hope. The old, nagging picture had returned—of a cramped, squalid boat; a dirty, sullen man; probably a slut of a wife to match. The thought of Christine in the hands of such people acted on her like a goad.

Twice more they did their five-mile stints, calling briefly at the occasional cottage, talking to the occupants of several more pleasure cruisers, questioning the few people they passed. For long stretches the towpath was empty, and at a place called Whixall Moss where the cut ran through desolate bogland, Hugh covered more than four miles without meeting anyone but a solitary peat-cutter wheeling home a sack of fuel on his bicycle. Clare made intensive inquiries at a village named Grindley Brook where there were nine locks in a row and where *Lucy* must have been held up for some time, but even here she was unable to find any trace of the boat. The canal, she realised, meant little to the people who dwelt near it; they didn't use it, or spend much time beside it, unless they happened to be anglers. Even so, it seemed extraordinary that no one should have remembered *Lucy* in all these miles.

Ahead of them, now, lay the last short stretch before the canal joined the Shropshire Union at Hurleston. It was becoming more and more probable that their quarry had left the Welsh section, and Hugh was growing concerned about what they were going to do when they reached the T-junction.

"We'll have to make up our minds whether they went to the left or the right," he said, "and it's going to be a difficult choice."

Clare was silent for a moment. Then she said: "You know, your last hunch about them came off pretty well— you said they wouldn't hang about on this canal and they obviously haven't. Try it again. Which way would *you* have gone at the junction?"

"Well," Hugh said, "it gets more industrial to the left, of course. If I'd gone up the Welsh section for peace and quiet, and only left it because I thought the place might get too hot for me, I should think I'd have been more likely to turn right, towards Autherley. We know it's mainly rural that way, and it's possible to get right through to the south without much trouble. . . . But then I might have had enough of quiet spots, who knows? It's all rather tricky."

"We could waste an awful lot of time if we made the wrong guess," Clare said.

"That's what worries me."

"Hugh, don't you think perhaps we ought to tell the police about *Lucy* after all? I expect they could find her quite quickly if they wanted to.

"Probably they could, but *would* they want to? We've still only a theory to offer them."

"Would we be any worse off if they refused?"

"We might be. It would mean breaking off our own search, and the explanations would be sure to take ages . . . I don't know . . . Let's get to Hurleston, first, anyway, and then we'll see."

The Junction was a green and tranquil spot at the foot of a staircase of deserted locks. There was a white direction post, and a solitary cottage facing the Welsh section, and that was all. They came to it late in the evening, having covered nearly forty towpath miles between them since dawn. They were physically exhausted, and very disheartened again by the continued absence of news. They had begun to think of *Lucy* as a sort of Flying Dutchman of the canals, and even to wonder whether the boy angler might not after all have made a mistake over her name.

They inquired at the cottage, but no one could tell them anything. Then Hugh spotted a brightly-painted houseboat moored against the bank a few hundred yards round the bend to the right and they dragged themselves along to it for a final call before abandoning the search for the night. There, against all expectation, they suddenly got wind of *Lucy* once more. The owner, after a moment's reflection, said that he *had* seen a boat of that name. At least, he said, he had seen a boat that had had L—U—as the first two letters of her name. A very old boat, with damaged paintwork, and the other letters hadn't been clear, but it had been a short name, so it was probably *Lucy*. She had passed his houseboat, he said, early on the previous day, heading south towards Autherley. Quickly, Clare asked him whether he'd seen any sign of a baby on board, but he shook his head. As far as he'd been able to see from his porthole, there'd been only one person aboard—a man. He couldn't describe him, because it had been coming on to rain at the time and the man had been struggling into an oilskin and sou'wester.

They thanked him, and turned away with very mixed feelings. It was a relief to have got on the track of the boat again, but otherwise the interview hadn't offered much comfort.

"Still only one chap by himself," Hugh said. "It doesn't look so good, Clare."

"If it was raining," she said, "the others would naturally have been inside."

"Well, that's true . . . At least it was a real stroke of luck finding out which way she went."

"It certainly was. She must have passed here just about the time that we were stuck behind the working boat."

"Pity she hadn't got a bit farther along," Hugh said. "We might have seen her. . . . It's interesting about the name not being clear—that's probably why no one could tell us about her. It simply hasn't been registering."

"And the fishing boy would have had a much better view, of course, because she was stationary."

Hugh nodded.

They took a step or two in silence. Then Clare said: "I wonder how far she's got, Hugh?"

"Well on her way to Autherley, I dare say."

"She's had two clear days, and it's an easy run on the Shropshire Union. She may have passed Autherley."

"She may, but I shouldn't think so—she can't be in a tearing hurry, or she'd have come faster down the Welsh section. Anyway, it's no good worrying—we can't do any more searching to-day. We'll probably catch her to-morrow, when we're fresh. Come on, let's get back to *Varley*."

They had scarcely started to ascend the path beside the locks when Clare came to a stop again. "Hugh—I've just had an idea. Wouldn't they have to show a permit or something at that lock at Autherley? We did."

Hugh frowned. "Why, yes," he said slowly, "I suppose they would. . . ."

"Then if we went there we could find out whether they'd gone by or not. It might save us a terrific amount of time."

"You're right," he said. "I should have thought of it. . . ." He broke off as a new thought struck him. "Clare, there's something else! They must have stopped to show a pass on their way up, too. The toll clerk may be able to tell us who was aboard *Lucy*!"

"Oh, Hugh, how stupid of us! Look, can't we go and see him right away?"

"We'll ring him," Hugh said. "It's quicker."

They found a phone box on the main road at the top of the locks, close beside the parked car, and Hugh soon got the number of the toll office from "Inquiries." But this time, their luck was out. It seemed that the regular toll clerk was away on holiday, at a place where he couldn't easily be got hold of by telephone, and the temporary man hadn't been around when *Lucy* had passed through from Gailey, so he didn't know who'd been aboard her. What he could tell them was that she hadn't come down again during the past two days.

"Well, that's that!" Hugh said, as he hung up. "At least it won't be long now before we know the truth about her—one way or the other. She's somewhere between here and Autherley, so we've got her!"

Before they turned in that night they made their plans for the morning. They would start from Autherley and work back, they decided, keeping themselves between *Lucy* and the lock. They would stick together, because the day's search was certain to end in an encounter, and there might be trouble. They would use both cars, parking one of them a suitable distance ahead before they set out on each leg, so that if they did happen to finish up miles along the cut, they'd have transport to get them back.

They were away early next day. They called first at Wheaton Aston lock, seven miles from Autherley, and left Clare's car there. Then they drove quickly to Autherley, which they reached soon after nine o'clock. They checked with the toll clerk that *Lucy* still hadn't been through the lock, and set off at once along the canal. The weather had turned cooler and they walked briskly, keeping in single file on the narrow path, with Clare a little ahead to set the pace. Neither was in the mood for talking. Both were tense with expectancy and hope.

They met no traffic at all for the first half hour. Then a working boat and butty came chugging through a bridge hole, with two pleasure cruisers following close behind. The first was new and rather lush; its name was *Curlew*, and it carried a party of young people, two men and two girls. The second was smaller and much less well cared-for, and there was a man in a sweater alone at the wheel. Hugh caught up with Clare, and they watched it closely as it drew nearer. Then a second man emerged from the cabin and joined the first. He was wearing a woollen bobble cap and he grinned happily as the boat passed. The name on the stern was *Four Winds*.

They pushed on fast, covering another three miles before they met their next boat, a short tubby one with a cruising couple aboard. A blonde young woman in vivid green slacks was sprawled on the cabin top, drinking in jazz from a blaring portable radio. The man at the wheel, very smart in a blue blazer with a crest on the pocket, eyed Clare with interest as the boat drew level and gave a friendly nod. "Morning!" he said, in a pleasant, cultured voice. "Lovely day!"

They returned his greeting, gazing after the boat as it slipped by.

There was a moment of shock—then Clare grabbed Hugh's arm. "It's her!" she cried, pointing to the peeling stern. "It's *Lucy*!"

Chapter Six

For a second or two they just stood and gazed after her. Clare could scarcely believe that all their efforts had gone for nothing, that the long chase had been no more than a futile irrelevance. But the gay music, the carefree girl, the man's nonchalant back seemed to leave no doubt about it. A look of utter despair settled on her face.

"You were right, Hugh," she said in a flat voice, "we've been wasting our time. They're just an ordinary holiday couple."

"Seems like it," Hugh said. "Of course they are. And now we're right back where we started—we haven't got a lead of any sort. . . . Oh Hugh!"

"Well, I don't understand it. . . ." Hugh had been building on this encounter more than he'd realised, more than he should have done, and now he felt as frustrated as Clare herself. "Hell, I know we didn't have anything very substantial to go on, but—all those coincidences. . . . It's really very odd. . . ." He began to move slowly after the receding boat, as though he were reluctant to let it out of his sight. Clare tagged along. After a moment he said, "You didn't happen to see into the cabin, did you?"

"No, there were curtains. . . ."

"And the cabin door was shut."

She nodded.

"And we wouldn't have heard anything from inside because of that blaring radio."

"But, Hugh—they're entirely the wrong sort of people."

"They're not the sort of people we've been expecting to find, I agree."

"They're not the kind to have sent that message."

"You wouldn't think so—but how do we know they didn't write it that way on purpose? I can imagine a tough, smart-aleck, ex-public school type being tickled to death at faking the thing to sound like his idea of Whitechapel. Just to mislead anyone who happened to see it."

"It doesn't seem very likely," Clare said—but unconsciously she quickened her pace a little.

"It didn't seem very likely there was a blonde aboard *Lucy* at one time," Hugh said, "but there is. And who'd have thought the dirty, sullen chap that boy described would smarten up into this one? Maybe other things aren't quite what they seem. . . ."

"Well, we can easily catch her," Clare said.

"I think we might as well. . . . After all, we've chased her for fifty miles—it's idiotic not to make sure."

By now the boat had drawn away and was several hundred yards ahead. They set off quickly in pursuit, but after two or three minutes she seemed as far off as ever.

"She must have put on speed," Hugh said, frowning.

"I'm sure she has!"

They were stepping it out now at a good five miles an hour, but the gap between themselves and *Lucy* was actually widening. They could still hear the radio, but only just. The blonde had left the cabin top and joined the man in the cockpit, taking over the wheel while he bent over the engine. The boat was certainly going much faster than it should have been. Hugh, pounding along, pointed to a long wet patch where water had lapped the bank and flowed over the towpath. "Look at the wash she's made!"

There was a bridge hole ahead, and they gained a little as *Lucy* slowed. But evidently she hadn't slowed enough, for they saw her stern slew round as her bows cannoned off the built-up side of the towpath under the arch. There was a thud, and a sound like the smashing of crockery. Then she was away again, along a dead-straight stretch, and the gap quickly opened out once more. Clare broke into a run. Hugh let her pass him and loped along behind. They could see the boat's wash clearly now, foaming away from the bows. They weren't gaining at all.

"She must be doing eight or nine knots!" Hugh gasped.

They ran for half a mile, but they couldn't keep it up. The towpath was slippery and treacherous where the water had flowed over it, and under the bridge arches there were old patches of soft mud that bogged them down. Once, gazing too eagerly ahead, Clare stumbled over a piece of jutting stone and narrowly escaped plunging headlong into the cut. Soon they had to drop to a fast walk again, and with sharp pains beginning to jab at them in unaccustomed places, even that was hard to maintain. *Lucy* was now no more than a speck in the distance. Hugh had been hoping she would be checked before long by the slower boats they had seen earlier, but the time-lag had been too great and there was no sign of them.

"We'll catch her at Autherley, won't we?" Clare called.

"Should do!"

But Autherley was still two miles away, and in spite of all their efforts the gap continued to widen. By the time they had the lock clearly in sight, the gates were already closing behind their quarry. Hugh could see the man in the blazer emerging from the toll office and walking back to the boat. She was already through when they reached the gates, swinging sharp left on to the Stour Cut, towards Gailey. The radio was still going full blast. The blonde had taken the wheel again, and the man was looking back at them. There was nothing in his attitude to suggest that he was at all perturbed. Hugh glanced across at the toll office and saw that the clerk was deep in a telephone conversation. Probably he'd stamped *Lucy's* permit automatically. Anyway, there was no point in stopping.

By now, the pace was beginning to tell on Clare. As Hugh turned to encourage her she called out, "Go on, Hugh, if you can! I'll catch you later."

"All right," he shouted.

He set off again at a fast stride. As he walked, he tried to remember what lay ahead of him. There must be six or seven miles of this cut before Gailey, with no checks apart from the bridges and the bends. After that, there was a whole string of locks, close together. He was bound to catch *Lucy* at the locks—she hadn't a hope of getting away. Her flight seemed pointless, if it was a flight. . . . But she certainly hadn't reduced speed. Hugh caught a glimpse of her once at the end of the long duckweed stretch, and hoped the weed would stop her, as it had stopped *Varley*—but it didn't. After that there were a lot of sharp bends, and the towpath became badly overgrown, and soon he had lost her completely. By now, he too was feeling the strain—he had covered ten miles at a trained athlete's pace and every step had become a struggle. There were knots of pain in the calves of his legs, and his feet were blistered; he was rolling and staggering from the fierce, sustained exertion. By the time he reached Gailey, he was moving at only a fraction of his earlier speed.

There was no sign of the boat at Gailey lock, but he knew that she couldn't be far ahead. One way or another, he would learn the truth about *Lucy* before many moments had passed. Hope and excitement spurred him on. He tore past a silent, deserted lock, and along a very short pound, a mere hundred paces, to the next one—and suddenly he spotted her. She was stationary in the lock. The top gates were shut, and the man was walking in a leisurely fashion towards the bottom gates, a windlass in his hand. The blonde was sitting in the cockpit with her feet up, paging through a magazine. There was a bottle of gin and two glasses beside her—evidently they'd been having a quiet drink. The radio, at last, was silent. The cabin door was wide open, and Hugh could see right inside to the forepeak, and there was nothing there of the slightest interest to him.

He knew, then, that there had been no flight—that it was the chase that had been pointless.

Sheer momentum took him to the boat's side. He was soaked in sweat, his hair was tousled, his shoes and trousers were covered with mud. His dry throat rasped as he tried to get his breath. The blonde glanced up from her magazine as he approached, and gazed at him in surprise. She was older than he had supposed, a woman of thirty or more, and a bit synthetic at close quarters—but her figure was good, and her face attractive in a brittle sort of way.

"Hallo!" she said. "My, you look hot!"

The man with the windlass came sauntering back. He was as tall as Hugh, and strongly-built, with dark curling hair and a lean brown face and an air of quiet assurance. He looked curiously at Hugh.

"Anything the matter?" he said.

Hugh shook his head. He suddenly felt very foolish. "I've been chasing you for miles—but it's all a mistake."

"*Chasing* us? Whatever for . . . ?" The man gazed at him intently. "I say, you're not the chap we passed back on the Shropshire Union, are you? With a girl?"

"That's right."

"Good God!—why, you must be absolutely worn out. We've been doing speed trials! What's the trouble?"

"We're searching for a—a lost baby," Hugh said.

"Really?"

"We had an idea she might be on board a boat called *Lucy*—that's why we followed you."

"I see. . . ." The man obviously didn't see at all—he looked completely bewildered. "Well, this boat's *Lucy*, of course, but I'm afraid we've seen nothing of any baby. . . . Perhaps there's another *Lucy?*"

Hugh shook his head. "We were just wrong, that's all."

"Is she your baby?" asked the blonde sympathetically.

"No—she belongs to the girl you saw back on the tow path."

"A young baby?"

"Not much more than a year."

"Heavens! How did she come to get mislaid?"

"Her father took her and hid her somewhere," Hugh said. "Her mother wants to get her back."

"I should think so."

The man still looked puzzled. "What gave you this idea about a boat called *Lucy?* It's none of my business, of course, but I must say I'm rather intrigued."

Hugh hesitated. "I'm afraid it's a long story, and I've bothered you too much already. . . ."

"No bother at all, old chap—I only wish we could help. . . .

Look, what about a beer or something? I should think you could do with one."

Hugh glanced back along the towpath but there was still no sign of Clare. She would hardly blame him, he thought, for not rushing back to her with news of a fiasco—and his throat was parched. "Well—that's very decent of you," he said.

"Come aboard. This is my wife, Brenda. Our name's Carruthers."

"Mine's Cameron," Hugh said. He stepped down into the cockpit and the blonde made room for him. It felt wonderful to sit down.

Carruthers said: "I'm afraid the beer won't be off the ice. . . ."

"As long as it's wet that's all that matters," Hugh said. He watched Carruthers searching for a bottle opener in a tray of cutlery. "You two have been up on the Welsh canal, haven't you?"

"That's right. . . . How did you know?"

"That's where we started to follow you," Hugh said ruefully. "You see, first of all we got the idea that this baby might have been taken on to a working boat, and when that flopped we switched to pleasure boats because someone mentioned a boat called *Lucy* that seemed to fit our picture. We picked up your trail on the Welsh canal, and we've been after you ever since."

"Sounds pretty gruelling," Carruthers said.

"Yes—we didn't have much time for the scenery."

"Too bad—it's a grand place up there. Not that we saw as much of it as we'd have liked ourselves, as a matter of fact. We got stuck with a spot of engine trouble."

"A *spot!*" Brenda said. "You never saw such a frightful mess—the boat was like a workshop."

"Couldn't get it right, either," Carruthers said.

"Only got it finally fixed yesterday. That's why we were putting *Lucy* through her paces to-day."

"She certainly goes pretty fast now," Hugh said wryly.

"Yes, I think I've done quite a job on her."

"When you ricocheted off that bridge on the Shropshire Union we felt sure you must be the people we were after."

"I'm afraid my wife's inclined to gawp when she's steering," Carruthers said with a grin. He began pouring the beer down the

125

side of the glass. "Sorry this is taking so long—the heat seems to have made it frothy."

"That's all right . . . Is *Lucy* your own boat?"

Carruthers nodded. "We picked her up cheap—not far from here, actually. She's still in a shocking state, but nothing like as bad as when we bought her—it took us a couple of days just to clean the old muck out of the cabin . . . Take a look inside, if you'd like to."

Hugh put his head inside the cabin. There were two settee berths, one on each side, and a folding table in the middle; a tiny galley; a roomy forepeak cluttered with boat's gear.

"Looks quite cosy," he said.

"Oh, she's all right for a holiday trip—bit cramped for anything else. . . ." Carruthers passed the beer, and poured out two gins and French for himself and his wife. "Well, here's luck!" he said. "Let's hope you find the baby."

"Thanks!" Hugh said. "Cheers!"

The glass was half-way to his lips when his eye was caught by something lying just inside the cabin door under the galley. He stared at it for a moment—then set the glass down and picked it up.

It was a fragment of a broken china beaker, and there was a picture of a rabbit on it.

Hugh looked at Carruthers, then at the blonde. They were both eyeing the bit of pot. Their faces showed curiosity, a faint surprise at his behaviour—nothing else.

He held it out so that they could see the rabbit. His heart was pounding, and he had to make an effort to control his voice. "Do you two usually drink out of children's mugs?" he said.

Carruthers's eyebrows went up a little. He took the fragment and inspected it for a moment—then handed it back with a smile. "The man we bought the boat from had a young family," he said. "This must have been there ever since."

Hugh regarded him uncertainly. "I thought you said you spent two days cleaning out the cabin!"

"My dear fellow," said Carruthers mildly, "anyone could overlook a bit of pot under a stove. It was probably stuck behind one of the legs. . . ."

At that moment, footsteps sounded along the towpath.

Hugh looked out, and saw that it was Clare. Without ceremony he left the cockpit and hurried to meet her. Her face was hot and flushed, and she was limping badly.

"Any luck?" she gasped, as he joined her.

"I'm not sure. . . . There's no trace of Christine, and they say they don't know anything about her. But I've just found this in their cabin." He showed her the bit of beaker.

She gazed at it, wide-eyed. "Hugh . . ."

"There's nothing else—the cabin couldn't look more innocent. No sign of a pram or cot, no sign of any clothes or toys—nothing. And their story is that this was left by the last people."

"I don't believe it. . . ." Clare took an angry step towards the boat."

Hugh restrained her. "Easy, Clare!—we've got to think this out. If they're lying, they're putting on a damned good act. They're quite unconcerned about everything. It's no good accusing them without any proof."

"If they've nothing to hide," Clare burst out, "why were they running away?"

"They say they weren't—they say they were testing their engine. They've got an answer to everything. . . . Besides, where would Christine be?"

"Couldn't they have handed her over to someone else before we saw them?"

"I shouldn't think that would have been very easy to arrange," Hugh said. "And why would they want to?"

"I don't know. . . ." Clare turned the bit of pot over and over. The break looked clean, but it was hard to be sure. . . . Suddenly she said: "Hugh, were they in sight all the time you were following them?"

"No—I lost them several miles back."

"Then mightn't they have stopped and hidden her somewhere?"

"I doubt if they'd have had time to hide all her things as well. There'd have been a frightful lot of them. . . ."

"They could have thrown them into the cut as they went along."

"That's true . . . I don't know how we'd ever prove it, though . . ."

He swung round sharply as the sound of a creaking ratchet reached his ears. Carruthers had left the boat, and was raising one of the bottom paddles to empty the lock. *Lucy*, it seemed, was about to continue on her way.

Clare could scarcely control her agitation. "Hugh, we can't let them leave till we know."

"They won't get far as long as they stick to the cut," he said.

"But will they stick to it?"

Hugh looked uncertain. "Maybe they won't. . . ."

"Hugh, if that man *is* 'A' and they *have* hidden Christine they'll abandon *Lucy* as soon as they get a chance and simply disappear. They could pick up Christine and start all over again somewhere else in a different name and we'd have lost our only link. It's now or never. We've *got* to stop them."

"There'll be a hell of a rumpus if we're wrong."

"We can't help that."

The second paddle was up, now, and *Lucy's*, cabin top was already sinking below ground level. Hugh still hesitated. Carruthers had been so plausible—and there was so little solid evidence. Just that bit of pot, actually—and that wasn't conclusive. It *might* have been overlooked. Yet there'd been something odd about Carruthers, too—he'd been milder than he should have been under provocation. And all those coincidences—the places and the times! And the way *Lucy* had cannoned off that bridge back on the Shropshire Union—that had certainly suggested flight rather than an engine test. Hugh suddenly remembered the crash of crockery. If the mug had been broken when they hit the bridge, they *were* lying. . . .

"All right," he said. "If we're going to have a showdown, we may as well get it over. Come on."

They walked quickly past the lock to the bottom gates. Carruthers was sitting on the balance beam, smoking a cigarette and watching the water level. He got up as they approached, and nodded pleasantly to Clare. "Hallo!" he said. "Sorry to hear about the baby."

Hugh took a deep breath and plunged. "Look, Carruthers—we may be making a bad mistake and if so we'll owe you a handsome apology, but the fact is there are one or two inquiries we'd like to make about you and your boat before we lose touch with you."

Carruthers stared at him. "Well, really . . ." His air of *bonhomie* had vanished. "You can't be serious."

"I'm quite serious. We're not satisfied about this bit of pot. I'd be glad if you'd hang on for a bit while we get things sorted out."

"There's nothing to sort out," Carruthers said sharply. "Not as far as I'm concerned. I've already explained about that mug—and I tell you we know nothing about any baby. It's too bad if you're in trouble but it's nothing to do with us—and quite frankly, old chap, I don't like your attitude. You're becoming a bit of a bore." He glanced down at the almost empty lock. "Okay, Brenda, any moment now!"

"If it's nothing to do with you," Hugh persisted, "at least you've nothing to lose by co-operating, and you'll be helping us a lot. Why not stick around till we've made our inquiries?"

"What inquiries?—and how long?"

"I'd like to get a telegram through to the Autherley toll clerk—he's away on holiday. He'll probably be able to tell us at once if there was a baby on board your boat when you passed through Autherley lock the first time." "He will, indeed!" Carruthers said. "He had a look over the boat. Send it by all means!"

Hugh was shaken. The man might have gone through Autherley lock on his own, of course, and picked up his wife and Christine afterwards. Or he might just be bluffing, playing for time. But his assurance was very disconcerting.

"You'll wait, then?" Hugh said.

"No, we won't wait," Carruthers snapped. "You can't expect us to hang about here for days while you prove your idiotic notion wrong—you seem to forget we're supposed to be on holiday."

"It won't take days," Hugh said. "It'll probably only take a few hours."

"Well, if you want us you can find us on the Trent and Mersey. You can bring your apology there!"

Hugh began to feel more cheerful again. "If you won't wait," he said, "there's only one conclusion we can draw."

"You can draw any damned conclusion you like." Carruthers leaned back against the balance beam, and the gate began to open.

"All right," Hugh said, "you leave us no option. . . . Clare, go back to Gailey and ring up the police. Tell them you want to charge a man with kidnapping your child."

Carruthers let go of the beam and advanced menacingly on Hugh, the windlass in his hand. "You're asking for trouble, my friend. Take my advice and clear off while you still can."

Hugh stood his ground, square and solid. "Go on, Clare."

Carruthers raised the windlass. Hugh ducked, and dived for his legs. In a moment they were rolling together on the ground, battering at whatever they could reach. They were equally matched in strength, but Carruthers knew more dirty tricks. Carruthers was desperate; Hugh was driven by weeks of pent-up anger and frustration. The struggle grew grim and bloody. Clare gazed around wildly, but there was no one in sight that she could call on for help. She tried to intervene, but the tearing, grunting figures were almost indistinguishable as they rolled over and over. For a full half minute they grappled and punched beside the beam. Then Carruthers was on his feet again, the windlass raised recklessly, and Clare gave a cry. Hugh flung himself out of the way, escaping the blow by a hair's-breadth. As he staggered up, Carruthers's fist caught him full in the face. He grabbed at the windlass as he fell back, and Carruthers held on, too, jerking him upright. For a moment or two they slogged it out with their free hands. A savage swipe from Carruthers landed on Hugh's neck and rocked him. Groggily, he struck out in return. Carruthers leaned back to avoid the blow—and, suddenly, it was all over. There was only emptiness behind Carruthers. He let go of the windlass in an effort to save himself, let out a yell, and disappeared over the side of the lock.

There was a moment of awful silence. Then Hugh staggered to the edge, and Clare joined him, her face ashen, and they gazed down fearfully, half expecting to see Carruthers's sprawled, unconscious figure lying on *Lucy's* deck. But he was all right—he'd missed the boat's stem by inches and was swimming, treading water. The blonde rushed forward with a shaft to help him. The bows of the boat were high and smooth, and there was nothing to hang on to, and for a while it seemed that he wouldn't make it and that Hugh would have to open the gate. Then he managed to wedge himself between the boat and the lock wall, and lever himself up, until he had his arms over the side and could clamber aboard. For a moment, he lay gasping. Then he looked up, his features distorted, and shook his fist. "By God, you'll pay for this!" he shouted. "I'll have you jailed. Open those gates, d'you hear?"

Hugh stepped back, wiping the blood from his face with the back of his hand and leaving fresh smears from his broken knuckles. "Well, that's that!" he said shakily.

"Oh, Hugh—you poor lamb! Here, let me clean you up. ..." Clare took his handkerchief and began to minister to him.

"I'm all right," he said after a moment. "Pretty lucky, too—if he hadn't gone over the side I don't know what would have happened. ..." He was still breathing hard.

"At least they can't get away now—they'll never be able to climb those slimy walls. ..."

"I know—but what are we going to do about them?"

"Hadn't I better go for the police?"

Hugh hesitated. "I suppose it's the only thing to do—though it's anybody's guess whose side they'll be on after this shemozzle."

"But, Hugh, we *know* Carruthers is 'A,' now—he'd never have behaved like that if he wasn't. ..."

"*We're* pretty sure he is," Hugh said, "but it won't be so easy to convince the police. That fellow's so damned glib—he'll say I started the rough house, he'll say I tried to detain him without any good reason. The police won't be sure about the rights and wrongs of the thing and they'll probably have to let him go while they investigate and then he'll give us all the slip, just the way you said. We're still not out of the wood, Clare. We need *evidence*. ..."

"There's the bit of mug."

"It isn't enough. We can't prove it was Christine's mug. We can't prove anything—not quickly. If only I'd been able to find just one thing that belonged to her. . . ."

He stared at the ground, frowning. The windlass was at his feet, and he stooped to pick it up. Suddenly he gave a sharp exclamation. "Wait a minute!—I've just thought of something. . . . That idea of yours that they might have dumped her things in the cut. . . ."

"You said we couldn't prove that, either."

"Perhaps we can! Look—we know they didn't dump anything before Autherley, don't we, because we'd have seen them. They probably didn't begin to think about it seriously until they were well into the Stour Cut—until they saw that I was still following them at the duckweed stretch. They'd have realised then that they hadn't a hope of shaking me off. They'd have started to get Christine's things together. They couldn't have chucked them overboard one by one, because some of them would have floated—they'd have had to pack up properly. They'd have kept going until the packing was finished—just a quick stop, somewhere, to dump Christine, and then on again, hell for leather. . . . But when I found them they were lounging about as though they had all the time in the world, as though they knew they were safe. Why did they think they were safe h*ere*? Why not the last lock? Clare, it's a chance. . . ."

Suddenly he turned and strode off to the top gates and fixed the windlass and began to raise one of the paddles fast. Water surged into the lock. *Lucy* moved quickly astern and hit the top gates with a crash. "Hugh! "Clare cried, "what are you doing? The bottom paddles are open—the water'll only run through."

"I'm going to drain the pound!" he said, and raised the second paddle.

After that, there was nothing to do but wait. The noise of the rushing water made talking difficult. Carruthers had started *Lucy's* engine to control the boat, and that added to the racket. He was gesticulating from the cockpit, he seemed to be shouting something, but they couldn't hear what he was saying. A great cloud of white suds was rising over the bows, as factory waste in the water was churned into foam. Soon the boat was almost invisible.

Already there was a big fall in the level of the short top pound. Stones along the banks were beginning to uncover, and in places the bare mud was visible. In the longer bottom pound the level was rising, but more slowly. There might be some flooding over the bank, Hugh thought but not enough to do serious damage.

Ten minutes passed, fifteen minutes. Then they started to walk along the towpath, away from the lock. All sorts of debris was emerging, now—rusty pails and glass bottles, tin cans, part of an iron bedstead, an old china sink. They examined everything, their faces set in concentration.

They were half-way along the pound when Clare cried sharply, "Hugh!—what's that?" and pointed.

It was something white, a dirty white, at the edge of the narrowing channel. A *bundle*!

Terror suddenly possessed her—unreasoning, panic-stricken terror. In a second she had dropped down on to the muddy stones and was ploughing knee-deep through the slime, with Hugh close behind her. Together they dragged the bundle clear of the water, tearing at the knotted sheet. Suddenly it split apart, scattering its contents. For a moment Clare rummaged wildly. Then she gave a long, sobbing sigh. There were things in the bundle—just *things*. Things that they'd wanted to find, too. They'd got their proof at last.

She watched shakily while Hugh spread them out. There were baby clothes, a tiny mattress, blankets and sheets, an eiderdown, toys. Hugh continued to grope around, searching for the weights that had kept the bundle down. Presently he found them—three squares of iron. They looked like ballast from the boat.

"Right," he said, "we've got all we need." He snatched up a soiled, crumpled nightie, and a piece of the ballast. "Come on."

They scrambled back through the mud and raced along the bank towards the lock. As they drew near, strains of music reached them. The radio was playing again. Astonished, they gazed down at the boat. The water was still, now, the suds had subsided, the engine was quiet. Carruthers had cleaned himself up and changed his clothes, and was sitting calmly in the cockpit with the blonde. They were both drinking gin.

Hugh gave a shout, and held up the nightdress and the square of ballast.

"Okay," Carruthers called. "We gave up long ago—I could have saved you all that trouble."

"Where is she?" Clare cried.

"In a little copse, a few hundred yards beyond Gailey."

On the instant, Clare turned and began to run. Hugh followed close behind her. They tore past the empty pound, past Gailey lock, past the string of cottages. Ahead, they could see the clump of trees. They reached it together and plunged in among the undergrowth. The cover was thin, but on the far edge of the copse there was a patch of holly, and they made for it. There, behind a bush, they found a small push-chair—and Christine, strapped in it, fast asleep.

Clare crouched down beside her, tears streaming down her cheeks. "Oh, my precious!" she murmured in a broken voice. "Oh, *Hugh*. . . ."

Chapter Seven

Some of the stray ends of the story were tidied up by Carruthers and the blonde later that day, when the police questioned them, but there were still several gaps and it was from Inspector Raikes that Clare and Hugh ultimately got the complete picture.

Carruthers, it appeared, was a fairly standard type of playboy crook. He'd been brought up in a decent family, he'd been expensively educated, he'd done well in the Army—but he'd never had any serious inclination to work. After the war he'd dabbled for a while in some racing car venture, and when that had failed he'd taken a temporary job as a motor salesman in a West End showroom. Then he'd discovered that he could use his charm to much greater advantage as a confidence man, and for several years he'd lived very comfortably on his wits and the private incomes of elderly women—though at the cost of two short spells in prison for false pretences.

Arnold Hunter had first met him through Peebles, and had run into him again—just out of jail and looking for any chance to make a bit of easy money—precisely at the moment when the plan to kidnap Christine was taking shape in his mind. He had been introduced to Brenda—who wasn't, it turned out, Carruthers's wife, but a casual girl friend with a police record of her own—and after a preliminary reconnaissance, negotiations had opened.

It was Arnold, glancing down an advertisement column in an evening paper, who had had the idea of a boat. Carruthers and the girl had both been attracted by the prospect of a summer holiday with pay. Carruthers had gone up to Gailey to take a quick look at *Lucy*, and—relying on his mechanical skill to deal with any engine trouble—had reported that she could probably be made to serve. Arnold had offered the pair four hundred pounds apiece for a trip of not more than three months, and after a little haggling over the cost of their keep they had agreed. The money, and all subsequent money, had been paid through a Birmingham bank where Arnold still had an account in a false name and with an accommodation address, dating back to one of his earlier illicit deals.

Carruthers had been the actual purchaser of the boat, and it was he who had carried out all the necessary preparations for the trip. Late one night he had moved *Lucy* out of earshot of Gailey, and next day he had got the engine going and tried her out for a few miles and moored her at a convenient spot near a road bridge just short of the first of the Wolverhampton locks. He had cleaned the boat and laid in stores, and then he'd telephoned Arnold to tell him he was ready and give him directions for getting to the bridge.

For several days Arnold had been keeping an eye on the mews, and on the Friday morning he had seized his opportunity. He had driven Christine to Wolverhampton himself. On the way he had stopped in north London to pick up Brenda, together with the bedding and baby clothes which she had bought on his instructions, ostensibly for a friend. Then he had driven straight to the rendezvous, had a quick word with Carruthers, dumped his load and returned at once to Hampstead.

That night there had been a heavy storm in the Wolverhampton district and *Lucy's* cabin had leaked like a sieve, soaking all the bedding. Christine had been peevish, and no one had got much sleep. To make matters worse, in the morning *Lucy's* engine had failed to start. Brenda, unused equally to boats and babies and not at all liking the idea of being stuck on a dirty bit of canal on the outskirts of Wolverhampton, had turned sour over the whole undertaking and had talked of packing up. Carruthers had told her not to be a fool, and had suggested they should ask Arnold for what he called "hard-lying" money. He had walked into town on the Saturday morning to buy roof-stopping and some new sparking plugs, tried to phone Arnold but failed to get hold of him, and sent off his impish message instead. Arnold had duly come up on the Tuesday and pacified Brenda with a bigger offer. By then, the weather had improved, the engine was working again after a fashion, and *Lucy* was ready to leave for the quiet reaches of the Welsh canal. The passage through Autherley lock had been made quite openly with Brenda and the baby aboard. What Carruthers had said to Hugh about that had been pure bluff.

From now on, until the final engine breakdown, everything had gone according to plan. No special efforts had been made to keep Christine under cover, but Carruthers had usually chosen a quiet time for going through the locks so that *Lucy* shouldn't come under too close scrutiny when she was stationary. He had made regular phone calls to London to report progress, and it had been on one of these occasions, when they were already well into the Welsh section, that Arnold had announced he was coming north in a day or two on an urgent matter, and the rendezvous at Llangollen had been arranged. No specific time had been mentioned for the meeting, and no exact place, so that when *Lucy* had broken down some twenty miles short of Llangollen there had been no way in which Carruthers could keep the appointment. He had considered ringing up all the local hotels, but had decided in the end that it would be safer to leave the initiative to Arnold.

When Arnold had failed to find *Lucy* near the town, his own dilemma had been acute. He had realised his danger, but he had realised too that if he went off to Ireland without making some new arrangement with Carruthers it would probably be only a matter of weeks before Clare got Christine again. His mood was desperate, and he had decided to take a chance and search the canal. When, on the second day, he had succeeded in locating *Lucy*, he had told the pair about the court order, and, to compensate them for any possible risk to themselves, had made an irresistible offer of large monthly payments for as long as they continued to have the child. There had been no long-term plans—at that time Arnold had still been hoping that Clare would give way and agree to go back to him. There had certainly been no idea that Carruthers and the blonde should take Christine over permanently—that had merely been Arnold's spiteful invention in prison. There had been a suggestion by Carruthers that he should take his temporary family to Bournemouth for the winter if nothing had been settled by then, but even that had not been definite.

After Arnold's arrest, Carruthers and the blonde had discussed many possibilities, including leaving Christine in some public place with a label tied on her and abandoning the whole enterprise; but the flow of money had continued and they had carried on from week to week without coming to any decision. They had felt reasonably safe from discovery until, on the Shropshire Union, Carruthers had thought he recognised Clare from a photograph he had seen in a newspaper. When she and Hugh had begun to follow *Lucy*, he had become convinced of it. After that there had been no alternative to jettisoning Christine and her belongings. The intention had been to collect her from the copse as soon as suspicion had been allayed, but beyond that nothing had been decided. . . . And that was the story. There was a strong probability, Inspector Raikes said, that the pair would ultimately be charged with helping Arnold Hunter to defy the law.

But much of this didn't emerge until quite a bit later. . . .

There was no hope that Hugh and Clare could return to London with Christine that day. The police had to be fetched, and Carruthers and his blonde taken back to the station, and Inspector Ellis Jones rung up at Llangollen, and long statements made. Then they had to collect Clare's car from Wheaton Aston lock, and Hugh had to go off and placate the canal authorities over the loss of their water while Clare bought some necessary things for Christine and rang up Lena to tell her the wonderful news. By that time it was too late to start for home and they drove back to *Varley* and made up a bed for Christine on the spare bunk. They were both tired out after the violent activity of the day, and soon after dusk they turned in. Hugh was asleep in a matter of seconds.

Clare lay awake for a while, listening to Christine's gentle breathing and marvelling at the adaptability of small children. She had expected, at the very least, a little fretting, but Christine had allowed herself to be nursed and fed and put to bed without a trace either of recognition or resentment. At that age, no doubt, kindness was all that mattered—just the feeling of being warm and safe. Perhaps kindness was all that mattered at any age. . . .

Clare thought of Arnold, who had known so little and shown so little. Her anger had died, now that she had Christine safely back, and all she could feel was sorrow that he had made such a mess of things. To be eaten up with hatred and malice was surely to create one's own hell? She would have been glad to help him, but the situation had got beyond that. One day, perhaps, if he ever showed any sign of wanting it, she would see him again. She could never be indifferent to what happened to him. But the old feelings for him were dead, stone dead—and now there was Hugh. . . . She gave a little sigh, and turned over and went to sleep.

Next day they packed up their things and drove over to Blampton to see Mr. Flint and arrange for someone to collect *Varley* and bring her back from the Shropshire Union. After that they had to call once more at the police station, and by now the story had got around and there was a knot of reporters eager for details of their adventure. But at last they were ready to leave and that evening they drove back to town in the two cars, with Christine comfortably tucked up on the rear seat behind Clare. It was late when they got in, and after a few cheery words with Lena, Hugh went on home, leaving the celebrations till the following day.

The morning was one of the happiest Clare could remember. Dressing Christine in her own clothes, getting breakfast for her in familiar surroundings, seeing her settle down with her own toys, was all pure pleasure. Clare found it wonderful, too, after all the frantic weeks, to be able to linger again over her own toilet; to luxuriate in a hot bath while Lena kept an eye on Christine; to varnish her nails and groom her eyebrows; to put on her most attractive summer frock, instead of those dreadful slacks, and choose at leisure the ear-rings that went best with it. She would have taken even longer if more reporters hadn't called.

After that the telephone began to ring and she was kept busy with messages of congratulation. One of them was from Mr. Harker, eager to hear the whole story from her own lips as soon as she had a little time to spare. Another was from Mr. Chappell—and he had a bit of good news of his own, because he'd managed to get a modest clerical job that he was very pleased about. Clare was delighted, and said that she and Christine would come round to see him as soon as the excitement had died down. In between the telephone calls she returned to the sitting-room and told Lena more bits of the canal saga that she'd just remembered, and watched Christine, preoccupied with her teddy bear in the playpen.

Hugh arrived just after twelve. His lips were still swollen and his face was badly discoloured round the eyes but he was in the best of spirits. At the sight of Clare he gave an appreciative whistle.

"I say, I say! Ready for work, are you?"

"Any time you like, Hugh."

"You look terrific."

"Thank you . . . I dare say you'll look all right yourself in a day or two!"

He laughed, and bent over the playpen. "And how's our trophy?"

"She doesn't know she's been away."

"Good for her. . . ."

Lena said, "Go and mix us a nice strong martini, Hugh. You know where everything is."

He nodded and collected some bottles from a cupboard, and went off to the kitchen for ice.

Clare said, "He still looks very battered, doesn't he?—it's a shame . . . He really was absolutely marvellous."

"I can't think how you'll ever repay him, dear," Lena said innocently.

Clare gave a faint smile, but said nothing. She didn't mind Lena's teasing. What had grown up between her and Hugh in the long days and nights of shared anxieties was pretty solid and established, and she felt no embarrassment.

"I think he was so furious he just didn't care what happened," she said. "It was really amazing the way he rushed in—I had no idea he was capable of it. I wish you could have seen him."

"I wish I could," Lena said. "It obviously does something to a girl!"

"What does something to a girl?" Hugh said, returning with the tray.

"Men, usually. . . . I've just been hearing for the third or fourth time exactly how you battled with the dragon."

"Oh, that!" Hugh grinned enormously. "Easy as falling off a lock!" He poured the drinks and handed them round.

"Well," said Lena, "here's to the happy reunion!"

They drank. Hugh pulled out his pipe and sank into a chair beside the playpen with a contented sigh.

Clare, watching her daughter lovingly, said, "You know, I don't think those two could have been so bad at bottom, or they'd never have bothered to get that rabbit beaker for Christine in the first place."

Lena laughed. "How like a mother! The enormity of taking the child at all pales beside the simple fact of their having bought her a painted rabbit! I expect it was an awful rabbit, anyway—they've probably corrupted her taste completely."

At that moment Christine pushed her teddy bear aside and reached through the playpen bars for Hugh's martini.

"See what I mean?" said Lena.

www.ingramcontent.com/pod-product-compliance
Ingram Content Group UK Ltd.
Pitfield, Milton Keynes, MK11 3LW, UK
UKHW040105010325
455690UK00002B/19